THE
and the
CAPTAIN

Trim the Cat & Matthew Flinders

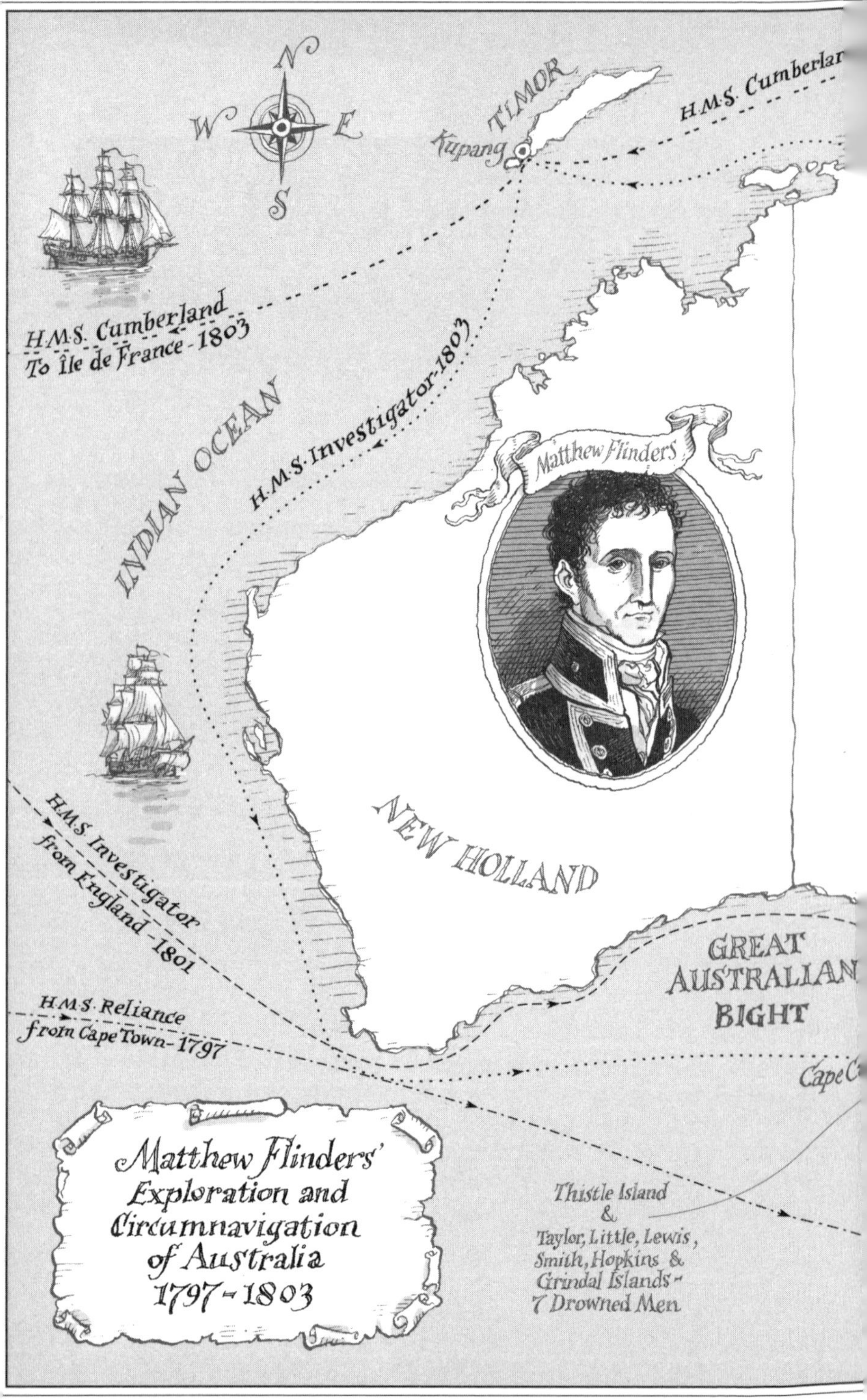

N
W
E
S
TIMOR
Kupang
H.M.S. Cumberlan
H.M.S. Cumberland
To Île de France - 1803
H.M.S. Investigator - 1803
INDIAN OCEAN
Matthew Flinders
NEW HOLLAND
H.M.S. Investigator
from England - 1801
H.M.S. Reliance
from Cape Town - 1797
GREAT
AUSTRALIAN
BIGHT
Cape C
Matthew Flinders'
Exploration and
Circumnavigation
of Australia
1797 - 1803
Thistle Island
&
Taylor, Little, Lewis,
Smith, Hopkins &
Grindal Islands -
7 Drowned Men

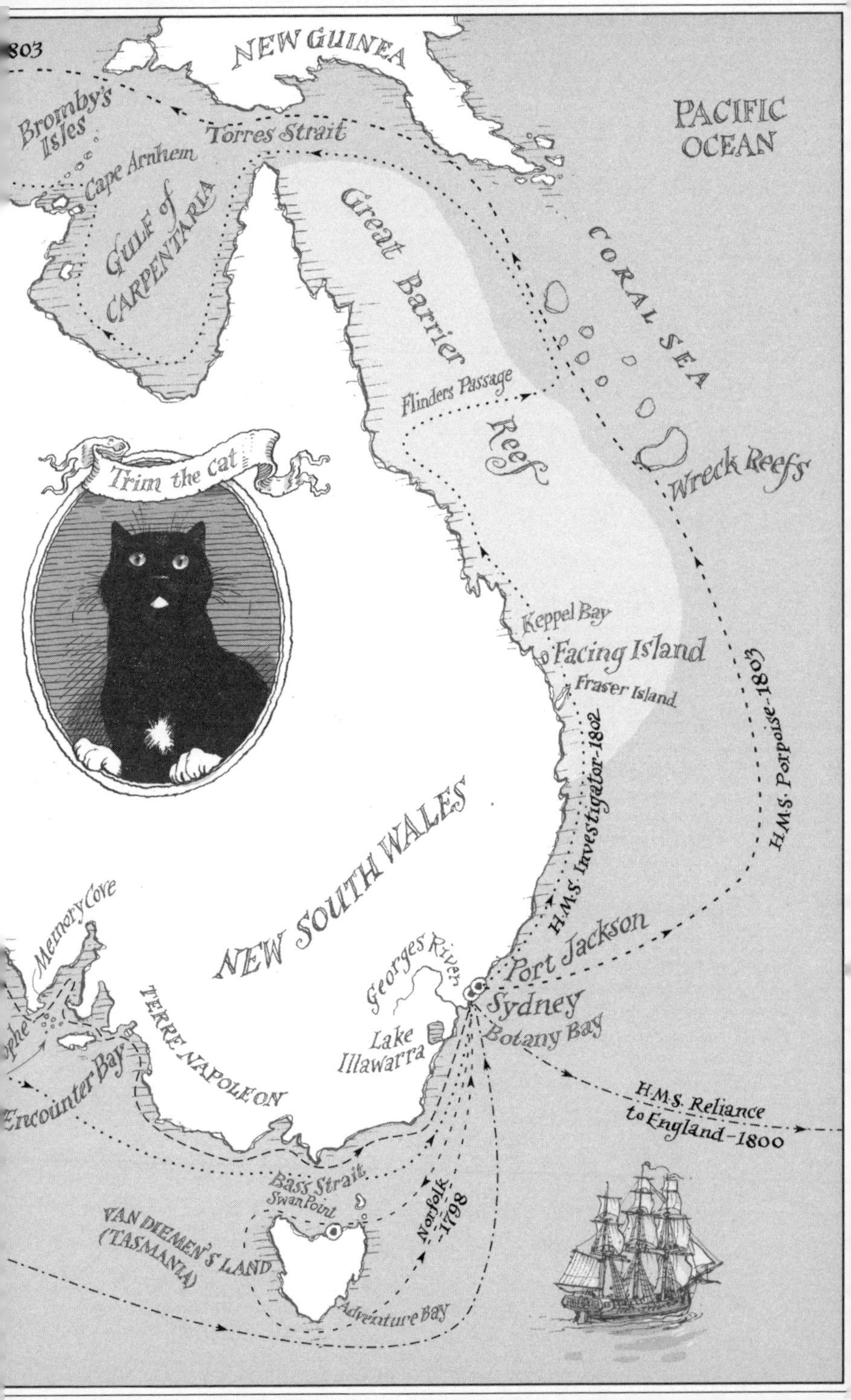
803
NEW GUINEA
PACIFIC OCEAN
Bromby's Isles
Torres Strait
Cape Arnhem
GULF of CARPENTARIA
Great Barrier Reef
CORAL SEA
Flinders Passage
Wreck Reefs
Trim the cat
Keppel Bay
Facing Island
Fraser Island
H.M.S. Investigator-1802
H.M.S. Porpoise-1803
NEW SOUTH WALES
Memory Cove
Port Jackson
Georges River
Sydney
Botany Bay
TERRE NAPOLEON
Lake Illawarra
Encounter Bay
H.M.S. Reliance to England-1800
Bass Strait
Swan Point
Norfolk -1798
VAN DIEMEN'S LAND (TASMANIA)
Adventure Bay

To Robin, David, Eric, Martha,
Mimi, Max and Isaac

First published in the UK in 2020
by Little Steps Publishing
Uncommon, 126 New King's Rd, London SW6 4LZ
www.littlestepspublishing.co.uk

ISBN: 978-1-912678-24-2

Text copyright © 2020 Ruth Taylor
Illustration copyright © 2020 David Parkins
All rights reserved.

The rights of Ruth Taylor to be identified as the author and David Parkins to be identified as the illustrator of this work have been asserted.

This book is sold subject to the condition that it shall not, by way of trade or otherwise, be lent, hired out or otherwise circulated in any form of binding or cover other than that in which it is published. No part of this publication may be reproduced, stored in a retrieval system, or transmitted in any form or by any means (electronic, mechanical, photocopying, recording or otherwise) without the prior written permission of Little Steps Publishing.

A CIP catalogue record for this book is available from the British Library.

Designed by Verity Clark

Printed in China
10 9 8 7 6 5 4 3 2 1

THE CAT
and the
CAPTAIN
Trim the Cat & Matthew Flinders

RUTH TAYLOR
Illustrated by David Parkins

Little Steps

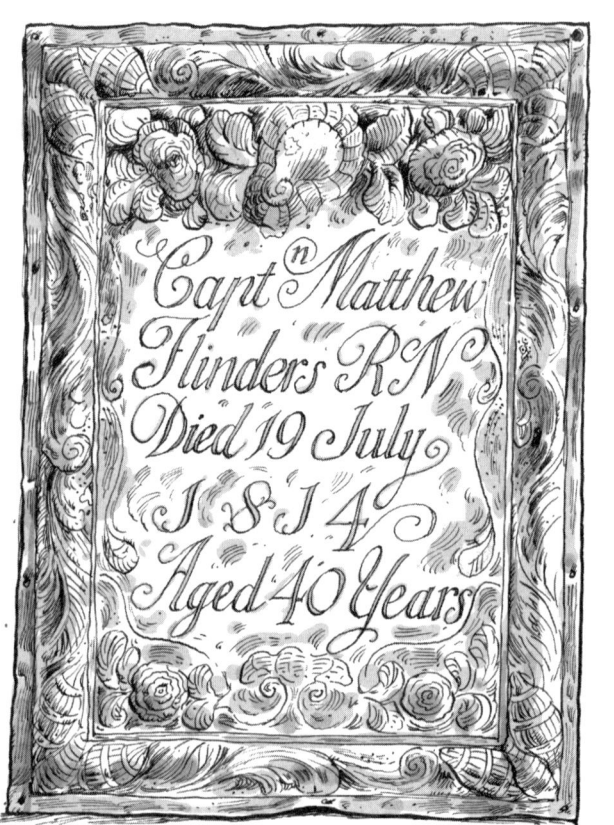

LONDON, January 2019

While gently brushing away the earth, the archaeologist slowly revealed a coffin with a lead plate attached to it that read: *Captⁿ Matthew Flinders, RN*. It was written in the curly writing of the 1800s and was surrounded by decorative swirls like tumbling ocean waves.

The great explorer, who had circumnavigated Australia and given it its name, was found lying among 40,000 bodies in the old St James's churchyard, behind Euston Railway Station. His grave had been lost for 160 years.

~ One ~

Since neither birth nor fortune have favoured me, my actions shall speak to the world.
— Matthew Flinders, in a letter to Sir Joseph Banks, 1804.

The wind whistled across the flat Lincolnshire fenlands on 16 March 1774, the day Matthew Flinders was born. He was the first child of Susanna Ward Flinders and Mr Matthew Flinders, a no-nonsense surgeon, pharmacist and 'man-midwife'. Mr Flinders probably helped deliver his baby boy in their grey stone house, which sat on the market square in the village of Donington, Lincolnshire. Mrs Flinders gave birth to nine more children, but only five survived – Matthew, Elizabeth, Susanna, John and Samuel. When Matthew was six he was sent to the nearby charity school, Thomas Cowley's, to learn reading, writing and Latin. He was lucky that his father was determined he should have a good education. What Matthew really enjoyed was arithmetic, in which he shone.

Matthew used to browse the Saturday market stalls opposite his house and wander around the town fairs that sold local hemp, flax and blue dye (woad). He couldn't have known how these common materials, so vital to the Navy for making sails, ropes and uniforms, would become part of his future life at sea.

Four months after his little brother Samuel was born, in 1783, Matthew's mother died, aged 31, of a fever. It seems that neither Matthew's father, who was not a trained doctor but a pharmacist, nor the local trained doctors could save her. We can only imagine how Matthew's feelings of loss and sorrow must have echoed his father's. He was just nine years old. Matthew's father wrote in his diary about his own distress 'at losing the dearest and most valued friend I had on Earth... My tears are plentifully shed each day. This world now has no charms left for me'. However, within a year he married an 'amiable' widow, Elizabeth Weekes Ellis, who took over the care of the children and the house. Elizabeth was a fond stepmother whom Matthew respected. Later, he would keep up a long correspondence with her during his many sea journeys. For Samuel, she was the only mother he knew.

When Matthew was 12 his father arranged for him to go to a small boarding school attached to the church in Horbling, 11 kilometres away, writing that it was time for the boy to 'be from home'. Matthew loved trigonometry, a branch of mathematics specialising in the study of angles. It stood him in good stead, as he would use it time and again when he surveyed the moon and stars, the oceans and land on his voyages of exploration.

During the school holidays Mr Flinders took Matthew to the annexe next to their house to teach him pharmacy in his chemist shop. He was preparing Matthew to follow in his footsteps as an apothecary (pharmacist). But the last thing Matthew wanted was to work in the medical field. He'd read an exciting novel called *Robinson Crusoe* by Daniel Defoe. It was about the thrilling adventures of a shipwrecked sailor on a desert island. Robinson Crusoe met enormous difficulties but showed such energy and imagination that he always managed to overcome them. Matthew wanted to be like him, and like his cousin, John, who had become a sea captain's servant at the age of 13. Matthew was open-mouthed at John's seafaring escapades. He set his heart on going to sea.

By that time the whole of Britain had heard the captivating accounts of Captain James Cook's daring voyages, exploring parts of Australia and the South Sea Islands never charted before. Matthew boldly told his father that he didn't want to be a surgeon. He wanted to be an explorer, and seek fame and fortune. Mr Flinders wrestled with his disappointment. His own father had been a pharmacist and surgeon and he'd expected that Matthew would carry on the family tradition. But seeing Matthew's determination, and considering that there would be one less mouth to feed, he agreed. 'I shall heavily miss him,' Mr Flinders wrote in his diary.

Proudly wearing his stiff new suit of naval clothes Matthew was ready to set off. In 1790, aged 16, Matthew waved goodbye to his family and took a horse-drawn coach to the Chatham naval base in Kent. He was assigned to HMS *Scipio*, a warship ready to patrol the English Channel. Matthew was set the tasks of memorising the names of hundreds of parts of the ship, of handling dozens of ropes and different sizes and shapes of sails, and of practising countless ocean-going procedures on the enormously tall sailing ship. He felt the cold salt spray on his face, swayed on the rigging high up the mast and balanced on the tilting decks. The smell of men's unwashed bodies; the taste of salted pork, often old and hard, with dried peas and ship's biscuits sometimes crawling with insects; and the sounds of rats and mice scurrying about the cargo were his daily fare for two months. At least he didn't feel seasick.

Luckily for Matthew his cousin, Henrietta (John's sister), was employed as a governess in a sea captain's house. Henrietta persuaded her employer, Captain Thomas Pasley, to take Matthew on board his ship. As soon as Matthew finished his training he started work as an able-bodied seaman on Captain Pasley's ship, HMS *Bellerophon*. He was paid £2 a month (worth about £60 today). *Bellerophon* patrolled the coastal waters around Britain looking for enemy ships. In the 1700s there was one war after another between the

British and, at different times, the Spanish, the French and the Dutch, all trying to be the most powerful. Many of Europe's navies toured their coastlines to prevent attacks. Matthew felt frustrated when he didn't see any fighting and after a month applied for leave to go home to Donington. He couldn't wait to see where his next voyage would take him.

~ Two ~

In 1789 there was a mutiny against Lieutenant William Bligh, the captain of HMS *Bounty*, in the South Pacific Ocean. The crew, angered by Bligh's harsh discipline, set Bligh adrift in an open boat with 18 other men. With extraordinary bravery and skill, Bligh and his men survived a 4000-kilometre sea journey to safety. When they arrived in England, 11 months later, the lieutenant was hailed as a hero. The Admiralty made him captain of HMS *Providence*, and commissioned him to take breadfruit from Tahiti to Jamaica as cheap food for the African slaves who worked on the British sugar plantations.

As soon as Captain Pasley heard about the plans, he recommended that Matthew apply for a position. To Matthew's great excitement he was taken on in 1791 as a midshipman – an officer of the lowest rank. The journey was going to last three years. 'God only knows what may be the event of such a long voyage,' Matthew's father wrote. Mr Flinders knew that going to sea was very dangerous. Few sailors could swim, there were no life jackets or special lifeboats, and many ships sank in stormy weather, crashed into rocks or were attacked by pirates who might murder everyone on board. Even if a sailor lost his grip and fell overboard he would be likely to drown. Matthew was 17 years old. He didn't think about the risks. This was his big chance to prove himself.

On board *Providence* Matthew found favour with Captain Bligh by being smart and reliable. Bligh trusted Matthew to calculate latitude and longitude, and to keep the watches and clocks wound up. This was essential for working out the position of the ship on the ocean and the distances it had travelled. Matthew was keen to learn as much as he could about navigation on *Providence*. The ship was accompanied by a smaller vessel, *Assistant*, which had 27 crew. Four men were marines, or naval soldiers, useful for keeping order if another mutiny threatened. *Assistant* was never out of sight of *Providence*, ready to help immediately if needed.

After sailing for six months, Matthew felt the thrill of looking out for the first time on the rugged green coast of Van Diemen's Land (now called Tasmania). He saw smoke rising from among the trees, which seemed to come from campfires. What he didn't know was that the local Aboriginal people had a warning system that announced the arrival of strangers by means of smoke signals. They had developed a well-organised society, having lived there for 40,000 years.

Bligh knew that Van Diemen's Land was a good place to stop for wood and water. He had anchored in the green waters of Adventure Bay several years earlier during the voyage of HMS *Bounty* – the voyage that had ended in mutiny. ('Van Diemen's Land' was the name chosen by the Dutch explorer Abel Tasman, who, in 1642, became the first European to see the land. He named it after the Governor General of the Dutch East India Company, Anthony van Diemen, who had sent Tasman on the voyage.)

When *Providence* anchored in the still bay no-one knew whether Van Diemen's Land was part of the mainland of Australia or not, as no-one had ever circumnavigated it. All ships that travelled from the Indian Ocean in the west to the Pacific Ocean in the east sailed around the south of it to get to the other side. Matthew's imagination was fired up as he thought about the discoveries waiting to be made by a bold navigator.

Bligh kept the ship in Adventure Bay for three weeks to take on fresh water and wood for fuel, and to put the goats, which were housed on board, out onto dry land to graze. Matthew wrote a detailed log of all the activities involved in looking after the ship.

When they arrived in Tahiti two months later, the local people gave them an enthusiastic welcome with singing, dancing, and gifts of bark cloth, fruit and pigs. They knew Captain Bligh from his previous visit before the mutiny on the *Bounty* had happened. It took three months for the breadfruit seedlings to be rooted in the rich earth of tropical Tahiti and made ready to take on board the ship. Eventually, 2126 breadfruit trees were collected, put into pots of soil and stored on *Providence* for the journey to Jamaica. This was the job of the two lively botanists, James

Wiles and Christopher Smith, both in their twenties. The two befriended Matthew. He was delighted to have the company of young men of similar age and education to himself with whom he could enjoy the tropical island paradise.

Providence took seven months to travel the 22,500 kilometres from Tahiti to Jamaica, via the Cape of Good Hope, arriving on 4 February 1793. Even the crew's water rations were cut to keep the plants moist. Some of the men were forced by thirst to sip the drips of water from the bottom of the plant pots. Despite all the botanical effort, the slaves detested the breadfruit and point-blank refused to eat them.

Because it took so long for sailing ships to cross the oceans, news spread slowly. A ship arrived in Jamaica later that month with the announcement that France had declared war on Britain. Captain Bligh was ordered to undertake wartime duties in the area. *Providence* and *Assistant* spent several months escorting naval convoys and capturing French ships. But Matthew felt impatient to get on with the scientific side of exploration, navigation and cartography, which he had practised under the guidance of Captain Bligh.

By June naval reinforcements had arrived, and Bligh received orders to sail back to England.

It was a relief for Matthew to be home. He wrote to Captain Pasley, who immediately invited him to take up the post of junior officer back on *Bellerophon*, which was still on war duties. Before taking up the offer Matthew carried a letter from James Wiles, his botanist friend on *Providence*, to Sir Joseph Banks, the immensely rich and famous botanist who had paid to be taken on Captain Cook's voyage to Australia and the South Seas between 1768 and 1771. Matthew didn't know then how important the meeting was going to be for his future. Sir Joseph Banks was not only president of the Royal Society (a society for the advancement of scientific knowledge), but he was adviser to King George III and to the British Parliament, as well as an active promoter of voyages of discovery.

On leave Matthew felt happy to be reunited with his whole family, including his two younger half-sisters from his father's second marriage, and Ann Chappelle, a special friend of the family. He was the centre of attention at social gatherings at home and in the surrounding villages as he recounted his tales of seafaring. At that time the family received the devastating news that Matthew's cousin John, recently promoted from midshipman to lieutenant, had died of fever on board his ship in the West Indies. He was 26 years old. Almost nothing was understood about illness then and there were no good treatments for most serious conditions, especially infections. The only treatments a ship's surgeon could offer for fever were immersion in a bath of tepid salt water, and cutting the patient to make them bleed. These often made them worse.

James Wiles asked Matthew to visit Sir Joseph Banks on another errand. He was well received. Banks had been involved in organising Captain Bligh's breadfruit expedition to Jamaica, so he knew of Matthew's position on board *Providence*. This was to Matthew's advantage. He was becoming known.

Back on *Bellerophon* Matthew, now a sprightly 20-year-old, experienced his first naval battle against the French under Captain Pasley. Europe had been thrown into turmoil by the French Revolution of 1789, and by the fear of the French army invading Britain and other countries to spread the revolution. Matthew's battle happened in 1794. The British called it the Glorious First of June. Over five days, 44 British warships fought 26 French ships in the North Atlantic

Ocean, 700 kilometres off the coast of northern France. The battle was a fury of deafening gunshots and cannon fire, the acrid smell of burning ships ablaze in billowing clouds of choking black smoke, crashing rigging, and wounded and killed seamen. Ships sank, taking with them hundreds of drowning men. After the terrifying battle, Matthew thanked his good fortune that he had emerged unharmed. However, he must have been shocked to see that one of Captain Pasley's legs had been so badly shot that it had to be amputated by the ship's surgeon. No anaesthetics existed then. A patient would be given alcohol or opium, but the effects were weak and didn't last, so surgeons had to operate with lightning speed. One French surgeon taught himself to amputate a leg in ten seconds; he had practised on 1000 dead bodies. In a live patient the surgeon would then have to stop the bleeding, which on board ship was done by applying boiling tar then stitching the skin together as swiftly as possible.

The battle was only called 'Glorious' by the British because they had won, but for the 8000 men who had been killed and wounded in battle it was far from glorious. For Captain Pasley, his seafaring days were over.

~ Three ~

Matthew's family were delighted when he returned home to Donington in July 1794. His two brothers, who had grown considerably since he'd been away, were enthralled by his stories of foreign shores and bloody sea battles against the French. Matthew's little brother Samuel, aged 11, decided he also had to go to sea. Matthew loved the company of his favourite sister, Elizabeth, who was 19, and his youngest sister Susanna, aged 15. However, the family was struggling to manage Matthew's middle brother, John, because of his rude and difficult behaviour. By the time John was 20 he had become 'deranged', according to Mr Flinders' diary, and had to be placed in an asylum in York, a hospital for people with severe mental difficulties. There he remained for the rest of his life, costing his parents £30 a year (£1100 in today's money) for his keep.

Very soon Matthew found out through one of the officers from *Bellerophon* that a ship was due to leave for Australia to take the new governor, Captain John Hunter, to New South Wales. Matthew applied immediately and was delighted when he secured the post of senior master's mate on HMS *Reliance*. He was passionate about exploring new lands and wanted to go further in his career as a mariner. It was this thrilling combination of adventure and opportunity that had inspired him when he'd read *Robinson Crusoe*.

After being repaired and refitted, *Reliance* sailed from the Deptford dock on the River Thames in early 1795 with Matthew aboard. Samuel, now aged 12, also joined as a 'volunteer'. This was a well-known way for a young boy to start his career in the navy. He was to be paid £6 a year (£850 today). Also on board was Bennelong, a senior Aboriginal man who had been captured on the orders of the previous governor of Sydney, Arthur Phillip. Bennelong was a member of the Eora people, whose land had been taken by the British to establish the convict colony at Port Jackson in Sydney Harbour. Governor Phillip had wanted to see if he could build good relationships with the local Aboriginal people by using Bennelong as a go-between. Bennelong had then been taken from Australia to England to meet King George III. There, suffering from London's bitterly cold winter weather, he had become seriously ill. *Reliance*'s surgeon, George Bass, nursed him back to health, so that by the time they arrived in Port Jackson he was well enough to rejoin his people. On the journey, Bennelong taught George some words in the Sydney Aboriginal language.

Once in Port Jackson, Governor Hunter used *Reliance* to transport supplies of food and animals from Cape Town in South Africa to Sydney to stock up the colony's food supply. The governor always struggled to provide enough food for the colony. In 1797 the South African dock workers and *Reliance*'s crew sweated and grumbled as they loaded three bulls, six calves, 100 merino sheep, a few goats, several cows and three horses on board. All were packed in like tinned sardines. The noise must have sounded like a farmyard with a fox loose.

While the ship was anchored, one of the lively ship's kittens fell into the water, swam to a rope that had been thrown by a sailor and clambered back on board. Matthew was so impressed with the little creature's bravery that he adopted him, calling him Trim, he wrote, after 'my uncle Toby's honest, kind-hearted, humble companion' – his servant. Matthew and the kitten had no idea of the adventures they were going to share. They would be the first to sail all the way around Australia, but they would also be shipwrecked, be taken prisoner by the French, find themselves completely lost, and eventually be remembered as great explorers 200 years later.

Reliance battled terrible weather from Cape Town back to Sydney. The journey took twice the usual time as the ship faced raging storms and mountainous seas. Matthew must have wondered if the ship was going to sink. All the animals were thrown about. Many were injured and others died. The waves and sea spray drenched the animals' stalls, and the sloshing up and down of the dirty water caused a terrible stink all around the ship. After 78 days *Reliance* eventually reached Port Jackson. With the gale-force winds and towering waves, the heavily laden ship had barely held together. She limped into port carrying the few poor animals that had survived, and in urgent need of repairs. It was a miracle that the ship had not sunk, taking everyone under the waves with her. (For hundreds of years, ships were called 'she' because generally no women were allowed on ships, and the captain of a ship would feel attached to and responsible for his ship as if 'she' was his wife. Sailors developed such a close relationship with their ship that they often hoped 'she' would protect them from danger, like a mother would.)

Safely back in port, Trim would rub his cheek against any sailor's leg until he was picked up and stroked. He became the sailors' favourite cat. Matthew wrote in his book about Trim: 'Trim believes that he is everyone's friend, and that everyone is his friend.' When no-one was looking the officers and crew gave Trim treats of meat and milk, which made him grow very quickly and very big. He developed into a truly handsome animal. He was as black as night all over, except for his four paws, which were as white as snow; his chest, which sported a white star; and his white bottom lip, which made him look comical.

Trim spent a lot of his time learning the things that a ship's cat ought to know. For athletic training the sailors taught him to jump high over their hands. To teach obedience they persuaded him to lie flat on his back with his legs stretched out straight and to stay there until he was told to get up. If he was left in this position for too long, he would make grumpy noises – 'Mrrr, mrrr' – while the end of his tail flicked backwards and forwards, backwards and forwards. This told the ship's men that he was uncomfortable and impatient, so they would give him the signal to spring up.

In Sydney, while *Reliance* was being patched up, with the permission and encouragement of Governor Hunter, Matthew used his time to practise map making and navigation, and to study hydrography (recording and analysing the sea and water conditions) which he had learned from Captain Bligh's good teaching. He also made exploratory journeys up and down the New South Wales coast. When Matthew had first arrived in Sydney, in 1795, there were no good boats to use. Private boats were forbidden in the colony in case convicts stole them and escaped. So Matthew and his friend George Bass, the young surgeon from *Reliance*, took *Tom Thumb*, an 8-foot (2.5-metre) open boat, to explore Botany Bay. Writing about George Bass, Matthew said that 'I had the happiness to find a man whose ardour for discovery was not to be repressed by any obstacles, nor deterred by any dangers'. He reminded Matthew of Robinson Crusoe.

Tom Thumb was tiny, no bigger than a boat that holiday-makers might hire on a boating lake, so Matthew couldn't risk taking Trim. Botany Bay was only 13 kilometres south of Sydney but the rivers running into the bay had not been fully surveyed. In October 1795, the two friends took great delight in rowing and sailing 32 kilometres up the Georges River (named after King George III, not George Bass) and back again, a journey that took them a month. When they returned to Sydney, they brought with them sketches of the river and a report about the fertility of the land surrounding it. Governor Hunter was impressed. On the basis of their survey he established a new branch of the colony called Banks' Town, after the botanist Sir Joseph Banks who had named Botany Bay in 1770 on his voyage with Captain Cook.

A few months later, the two men set off

enthusiastically to explore a large river a few kilometres further south. This time they ran into trouble. The current was so strong that it took the boat further along the coast than they wanted. When they tried to land on a beach, large waves flung the boat onto the shore, causing all their clothes, provisions and guns to be soaked with sea water and filled with sand. Before long, two Aboriginal men came to investigate. Matthew and George were able to make themselves understood. They indicated that they were looking for fresh water.

Their Aboriginal guides took them to a river that emptied onto the beach. At first the two guides got into *Tom Thumb*, but the river was so shallow that they had to climb out of the boat and walk alongside it as the boat made its way upstream. They were taking the two Englishmen towards Lake Illawarra, a large lagoon that fed the river a few kilometres away. Soon more Aboriginal men appeared until there were about 20, with others still arriving. Matthew and George started to feel nervous.

On the beach Matthew had trimmed the long, tangled hair and beards of the Aboriginal guides. The two men who had benefitted from Matthew's barber-shop skills now persuaded their comrades to submit themselves to the same treatment. Matthew took out a large pair of scissors and started to shear the beards and hair of the other members of the group. Some of the younger men screwed up their faces in alarm to see such a dangerous-looking instrument straying so close to the other men's noses, but they eventually joined in when they saw the results.

Matthew and George felt increasingly anxious as the Aboriginal people 'had the reputation in Port Jackson of being exceedingly fierce, if not cannibals' (man-eaters). Matthew and George didn't know that this wasn't true, which is why they decided not to spend more time trying to reach the lagoon. They persuaded their guides to show them a place nearby where they could dig down to find fresh water, and they gratefully filled a cask with 35 litres.

They returned safely to Port Jackson, and in 1798 the governor allowed them to take a small sloop, *Norfolk*, a sailing ship about the size of a ferry. With eight volunteer crew members they were able to explore much further down the south-eastern coast of Australia. Governor Hunter's instructions were to travel on to Van Diemen's Land to see if there was a sea channel between it and Australia. Until then it was thought to be one continuous land mass.

This time Trim kept them company. He showed a fascination for the special instruments Matthew used on deck to look at the positions of the moon and stars. Trim would stare at the moving hands of a large watch held in Matthew's palm. He would reach out a paw to touch the watch's second hand, the fastest moving hand on the watch, listen to it ticking and, appearing unsure whether it was alive or not, walk all round it, meowing.

Matthew explained the watch to his cat. 'You see, Master Trim, are you listening now? I measure our distance down the globe by the angles of the moon and stars to us. It's called latitude.'

'Meow,' Trim said.

'And to measure where we are, east or west of that line, I use the difference between the time in England on my watch, and the time here by the sun's shadow. Are you following me?'

'Meooow,' replied Trim.

'We call that longitude. With all your learning, sir, you'll soon be a lieutenant like me.'

It was a very complicated calculation. When Matthew finished he would call out 'Stop', which was the sign for Trim to run up the ship's rigging, meowing his observations from high up on the topsail, his fur ruffled by the wind.

As well as the hundreds of kangaroos, seals and seabirds they saw on their journey, the men witnessed a particularly extraordinary sight. Along the east coast of Van Diemen's Land, they saw a massive flock of 'sooty petrels' – short-tailed shearwaters, which are dark brown seabirds related to the albatross. Matthew recorded that the flock was more than 70 metres deep and 250 metres wide, and that the birds were 'flying compactly ... for a full hour and a half'. In his journal, he wrote that there must have been at least 100 million birds. He might have thought he was going to have a huge dinner. The men often shot birds, including shearwaters, and other animals for fresh food. One day they shot enough for each man to eat nine birds. Today the short-tailed shearwaters are on the edge of being an endangered species.

After three months of exploration, as *Norfolk* rounded the north-west coast of Van Diemen's Land, shouts and laughter broke out. They had finally shown without doubt that there was a precious sea lane between the mainland of Australia and Van Diemen's Land. Matthew, George Bass and the crew toasted each other with their generous rum ration (285 millilitres each per day) in 'joy and congratulations'. Perhaps Trim was given a piece of baked black swan from one that they had caught at Swan Point on the north coast.

When they returned to Sydney, Matthew asked Governor Hunter to name the channel Bass Strait. Sailing through the Strait would take a full week off the journey from the Great Australian Bight in the west to the Tasman Sea in the east. This saved valuable time, reducing by nearly 1000 kilometres the trading route of ships travelling from South Africa or India bringing livestock, tea and rice to Sydney. Before this, ships had taken the long way around the southern tip of Van Diemen's Land, believing it to be part of mainland Australia.

The thrill of discovery was all Matthew needed to set his heart on becoming a professional explorer. He knew that there was so much more to be learned about the Australian coast. His main problem was that there weren't any ships big or strong enough in Sydney to make a long and difficult journey around the continent.

The year was 1800. Sydney, the only town in Australia, was very small. It had been built on Sir Joseph Banks's recommendation as a settlement for British convicts only 12 years previously. Governor Hunter was finding it hard to feed, clothe and house the people, and keep the colony in good order. The ship *Reliance*, like all sailing ships of the period, was made of wood, and its timbers had started to rot. It was now seven years old and it let in a lot of sea water. It could no longer be relied upon. Many wooden sailing ships only lasted ten years. Matthew realised he would have to obtain a good ship from England. He struck on a plan. He would go home and present all his charts and observations to Sir Joseph Banks. These would support his proposal for one or more seaworthy ships to be made available to him to continue exploring Australia. He felt sure Banks would admire his work.

By February 1800, all the repairs to *Reliance* were complete. She was stocked with food, drink and animals for the five-month journey back to England. Matthew must have breathed a big sigh of relief when the ship finally left Port Jackson on 3 March.

He carried Trim on board. Soon Trim was enjoying his favourite game, which was chasing a musket ball. This was a small lead ball used in the ship's guns, which were kept ready in case pirates attacked. One of the sailors would attach a string to the ball and roll it around the deck for Trim to scamper after. When it stopped Trim would pat it hard with one of his paws to keep it moving, often making it follow a circular path on its string. Matthew concluded that Trim was experimenting in astronomy (the science of moving bodies, like the Earth and the Sun). When two sailors placed themselves at each end of the deck and rolled the musket ball backwards and forwards, Trim ran after it like a rugby player, pouncing on the ball and throwing himself on his side as he tried to clutch it between his front and back paws. He didn't stop until the sailors stopped. Then he would flop down on his belly, panting and purring.

Soon after they sailed from Port Jackson, one of the sailors heard something unusual. He called Matthew, who picked up his musket. Without making a sound they crept down into the hold of the ship where the stores of food, beer and musket balls were kept. They saw two strange men wearing coarse striped convict shirts and trousers with arrows printed on them. 'Up!' was all Matthew said, pointing his musket towards the stairs.

These were convict stowaways from Sydney, and Matthew was secretly pleased to have found them.

Normally they would have been flogged or thrown overboard, but he immediately set them to work pumping out the water that was already leaking into the ship at a rate of 26 centimetres every hour. This way, not only did the convicts earn their keep, but because of their good behaviour they were overjoyed to become free men when the ship arrived in England five months later.

~ Four ~

Once *Reliance* had anchored in the naval dockyard at Deptford on the Thames, Matthew managed to find a good woman, Mrs Pilkington, who lived in the port, to take care of Trim. He then took the coach to central London on his mission to obtain a ship.

Trim was not at all used to living on dry land, and especially not in a house. Mrs Pilkington could not possibly have known what she had taken on. On the top floor Trim found an open window from which he could go out onto the rooftops and watch for Matthew's return. When it rained, Mrs Pilkington always shut the window. For most cats this would have put an immediate stop to getting back in, but not for Trim. One day he dashed at the window with such speed that, with an enormous crash, 'he bolted through the glass like a clap of thunder', Matthew wrote. The tremendous din frightened Mrs Pilkington out of her skin, and she went to see what had happened.

'Good grief Trim, it's *you*! *My*! What have you done? Have you cut yourself?'

Luckily Trim had burst through the window without any sign of injury.

'Captain Flinders said you were an extraordinary cat. Now I can see why!' said Mrs Pilkington. She liked to call Matthew 'Captain Flinders'. It sounded grand. She didn't know that it would be another ten years before he would be promoted to captain.

'But you know, Trim, I'll have to keep you indoors from now on in case you go breaking through other people's windows, and get yourself arrested as a burglar.'

One day Trim heard a mouse scratching inside the cupboard that held Mrs Pilkington's best china. Without hesitation he flew into it like a storm. Bits of cups and saucers flew in all directions. There was no stopping Trim until he'd caught that mouse. Hearing the terrible racket Mrs Pilkington thought that some hobgoblin must have been making mischief in her cupboard. She opened the door wide in fear just as Trim flew out and jumped onto her shoulder.

'Argh! You devil!' she shouted, nearly dying of shock. Seeing her best crockery smashed to bits, she was just about to give Trim a thorough walloping, whereupon Trim, instead of running off, rubbed his whiskers against her chin and purred. Mrs Pilkington couldn't bring herself to beat Trim. She heaved a big sigh, put Trim down and started picking up the precious pieces.

At the end of the week Matthew arrived at the house to collect Trim. Mrs Pilkington sat him down and, over a cup of tea, told him all about Trim's alarming antics. Trim was already standing on Matthew's shoulder purring, but Matthew put him down and spoke sternly to him, wagging his finger.

'Master Trim, I expect much better of you than this.' Trim rubbed his cheek along Matthew's finger. Before leaving, Matthew paid Mrs Pilkington £1 (equal to £80 today) for the broken window and china, and for looking after Trim.

Matthew and Trim set off for London in a coach pulled by four big horses. Trim stretched out his fine white paws in his usual lion pose, and the two gentlemen passengers sitting opposite glanced at him admiringly. They were so fascinated by Trim that for the whole journey they asked Matthew questions about his education, manners and adventures. Matthew boasted of Trim's mastery of seamanship, astronomy and etiquette. When they arrived in London the two gentlemen shook Trim's paw and patted his head, saying 'Charmed, I'm sure, sir' as they left the coach.

It took six months for the Admiralty to finally agree to provide Matthew with a ship. Imagine his excitement at taking charge as the commander of a newly refitted ship called HMS *Investigator*. The Admiralty's instructions for his expedition, running to 13 long pages, ordered not only the mapping of Australia's entire coastline, but the recording of the wind and weather, tides, sea depths, rivers, harbours and inlets, where to safely drop the anchor, latitude and longitude, fertility of the soil, native customs, vegetation, wildlife and much more.

Sitting at their desks in London, the men of the Admiralty couldn't possibly have known how much work they were instructing Matthew to undertake.

To begin with, Australia is much larger than Europe. At that time, it had an unknown coastline of more than 26,000 kilometres. However, the Admiralty did know how dangerous it was to sail into uncharted waters, and how hundreds of ships were wrecked or sank every year, many without trace. They also knew that most sailors couldn't swim. Many hundreds of sailors drowned with their ships, and even more died of diseases for which there was no effective treatment. Although cork lifebelts had been invented, they weren't used, and there were still no special lifeboats. The ships simply carried, or towed, one or two small boats that could be launched by the sailors in an emergency.

The first European to ever land in Australia had been the Dutch explorer Captain Willem Janszoon in 1606. The Dutch explorers called Australia 'New Holland'. However, when Captain Cook charted the east coast of Australia in 1770, he claimed the whole country for Britain, naming the eastern half 'New South Wales'. Captain Cook had instructions from the Admiralty to 'take possession of Convenient Situations in the Country in the name of the King', with the consent of the inhabitants. But how could the inhabitants – the Aboriginal people – possibly have given their consent without a common language and compatible laws? They weren't asked.

The Admiralty's main reason for agreeing to Matthew's case for another exploration was that almost nothing was known about the continent of Australia. No-one knew whether it was one big land mass or two islands, and the massive interior of the country was still a mystery. The French, who wanted to claim parts of Australia for France, had already sent an expedition there in October 1800, giving Matthew a sense of urgency to set off on his own voyage.

Matthew realised that this was his big chance to be famous – perhaps almost as famous as Captain James Cook.

In January 1801, with great pride and a strong sense of purpose, he stepped on board *Investigator* with Trim in his arms. Trim made himself at home straight away. The new sailors were as delighted with his tricks and affectionate purring as the *Reliance* crew had been. But what Trim was not expecting was for *Investigator* to be home to four dogs. Without delay he let them know who was boss. When the dogs played together on deck, Trim would walk right into the centre of the pack to box the ear of one and scratch the nose of another. They soon learned to clear a path for him. More than once Matthew sent Trim to the back of the ship to move the dogs out of the way. Trim would run briskly halfway along the deck, crouch down like a panther stalking his prey, then boldly walk up to the leader of the pack and strike a blow on his nose with a threatening 'Meow!' If the dog did not back off Trim flew at him with his war cry: 'Yowou!' And if the dog still didn't move away Trim jumped up on the handrail above the dog and rained down so many blows on his head and face that the dog would run off with his tail between his legs, yelping. 'Trim was the undisputed master of them all,' Matthew wrote.

Matthew would spend the next six months on the demanding task of preparing the ship and the 83 crew at the dock in Sheerness, Kent, for their long and dangerous journey. A dozen instruments for navigation and surveying were loaded. Many copies of previous charts, maps and journals were unpacked. They included the first map, Willem Janszoon's of 1606, and those of 20 other European explorers, including Captain Cook, sailors who had all completed maps of disconnected parts of the coast with varying degrees of accuracy. Matthew took plain journals to use as diaries, three types of ink and 2000 quills for his pen. Sir Joseph Banks, now Matthew's supporter, had given him the gift of 18 volumes of the *Encyclopaedia Britannica* for his bookshelf.

On board *Investigator* were a naturalist, an astronomer, two artists, a gardener and a miner, plus four of their servants. With no refrigeration the ship was stocked with dried, pickled and salted food to last 12 months. In stalls of straw the ship also housed live pigs and sheep, as well as geese and other birds to be eaten on the voyage. Sheep's milk might have been available, and would certainly have been enjoyed by Trim. With hardly any space left, Matthew removed ten cannons to make way for ten tons of extra water. The Admiralty supplied 'presents' for 'the native inhabitants'.

A smaller ship, *Lady Nelson*, was sent on ahead to Sydney, specially stocked with an extra 12 months of provisions so *Investigator* could complete the charting of any remaining coast. The final document delaying Matthew's departure was a safe passage passport from the French government. He didn't know that the Admiralty hadn't yet asked the French for it. England was at war with France, so the passport was essential to prevent fighting if he came across French ships at sea, or problems in a French port. But, of course, the French government was occupied with the war, not with Matthew's passport.

At the same time Matthew met up with Ann Chappelle, the family friend to whom he had been writing for several years. He was 27 years old and wondering whether or not to marry. He wrestled with the idea of marrying Ann, a young woman he had become very fond of, but his concern was that he had little money and his future career was not secure. He wrote to his father asking for a loan so that he would be in a better position to support Ann, but his father refused, writing in reply: 'it cannot be a hard Task for a grown person … to obtain their own support'. Ann was herself unsure, not least because her own father, a sea captain, had died at sea when she was four years old, as had two of her uncles. However, Ann was 30 years old, she liked Matthew and he was an attractive proposition as a husband. She was keen to obtain his assurance that if they married they wouldn't be separated from each other. In their discussions about marriage Matthew even suggested taking Ann with him to Australia. On an impulse, his leaving date approaching, Matthew wrote to Ann that he would soon be in London: 'If thou wilt meet me there, this hand shall be thine for ever.' Matthew and Ann married, not in London, but in Ann's home village of Partney on 17th April 1801.

Ann excitedly packed her luggage. When she boarded *Investigator*, she began to settle herself into the large cabin reserved for Matthew as commander. Ann was eagerly looking forward to the journey of a lifetime and being together with her new husband. But when the Navy Board found out that the commander's wife was with him, they forbade it. It was against the rules. Matthew tried to persuade them but they wouldn't budge. With heavy hearts, Matthew and Ann had to part. Saddened and frustrated, Ann returned to her family. She had only been married for seven weeks. Ann and Matthew didn't know that they wouldn't see each other again for nine long years.

~ Five ~

Matthew must have been feeling increasingly frustrated waiting so long for his French passport. Eventually, after four months, it arrived. *Investigator* weighed anchor and left Sheerness in July 1801, her sails filled with wind and Matthew filled with hope. However, it wasn't long after the ship left that his excitement turned to dismay. He wrote in his journal that 'we had the mortification to find the ship beginning to leak'. About seven centimetres of water was entering the ship per hour. Matthew felt cheated. The Admiralty had told him that no better ship could be spared, and he hadn't felt that he could refuse the one offered. Not only was water coming in, but the masts were found to be rotten and the rigging was faulty. At the first stop, in Madeira, *Investigator* was held up for urgent repairs for five days. Water, wine, beef, fruit, vegetables and tobacco were purchased. Matthew even felt aggrieved that wine and meat were very expensive. 'I therefore took only small quantities of each,' he wrote.

The ship sailed on, taking three months to reach the Cape of Good Hope in South Africa. By then more repairs were needed. The wooden seams once again had to be sealed against water leakage with caulk, a mixture of tar and sheep's wool. While the torn sails were being repaired, fresh meat, oranges and lemons were brought on board. For 50 years it had been known that oranges and lemons prevented scurvy, a terrible illness suffered by sailors. Scurvy caused very painful weeping skin sores, loose teeth and such severe tiredness that sailors lay helpless in their hammocks. Old wounds re-opened and healed fractures broke again. Sailors didn't know that scurvy was caused by a lack of vitamin C – that wasn't discovered for another 120 years. But they knew that fruit and vegetables, which often couldn't be obtained or kept fresh on long journeys, prevented and cured scurvy. Sailors on Captain Cook's voyages avoided the illness by eating pickled cabbage. When the crew saw that it was served only to the officers they demanded it too. At that time it was not known that drinking large quantities of alcohol every day reduced the benefit of vitamin C. More sailors died of this agonising disease than from shipwrecks, storms, warfare and all other diseases put together. Historians estimate that over 2 million men died of scurvy between 1570 and 1870, when steam ships took over from sailing ships.

Five months after leaving the Cape of Good Hope, on a clear day, Matthew was excited by the sight of the wooded south-west coast of Australia where his mission was to start in earnest. For the next six months he and his crew painstakingly followed the instructions of the Navy Board. They surveyed and charted the south coast of Australia from west to east, and made detailed observations and drawings of the land, sea, wildlife and Aboriginal peoples. They had a journey of 6400 kilometres ahead of them before they could rest in Sydney.

On 21 February 1802, Matthew instructed *Investigator*'s master, Captain John Thistle, to take a small boat they kept on board, called a cutter, and six seamen to sail to a nearby island. They were near what is now called Port Lincoln in South Australia. It was urgent they find a safe place for the ship to anchor for the night, and to fetch much-needed fresh water. The men finished their task, and were seen moving about on the beach and getting into the cutter ready to return. On the way back to the ship, the cutter suddenly disappeared from view. After half an hour it had not arrived. The sun was going down, the light fading, the shadows merging to blackness. Matthew, feeling anxious about the men's fate, sent his second-in-command, Robert Fowler, in a rowing boat with an oil lantern to look for the seven men. After two hours Fowler had not returned. The crew strained their eyes towards the shore. A gun was fired and soon afterwards Fowler appeared. He had found no trace of John Thistle and the six crew, but in the area where they had last been seen, Fowler's boat had nearly capsized in a violent current. Matthew knew that only two of the men in the cutter could swim, and he had seen the grey glint of sharks' fins gliding through the water. Could the men have been eaten by sharks?

For the next three days Matthew and his men, feeling worried and upset, made seven thorough searches on the sea and the shore. Broken timbers of the cutter were discovered in the surf, but none of the men. In the fine, yellow sand Matthew found a small rum keg that had belonged to John Thistle, but not one of the men was ever found. Matthew felt devastated. The loss of 'our unfortunate shipmates', Matthew wrote, was 'heavily felt'. He was particularly fond of John Thistle, who he had known for eight years. Matthew thought he was 'truly a valuable man, as a seaman, an officer, and a good member of society'. Thistle had been with him when he and George Bass had sailed around Van Diemen's Land three years before. 'His loss was severely felt by me; and he was lamented by all on board.' Matthew could hardly believe that seven men could have been lost in the blink of an eye. The lead weight of a commander's responsibility bore down on his shoulders. Matthew named the area Memory Cove, the nearby headland Cape Catastrophe, and seven local islands after each one of the seven drowned men. The islands keep their names today.

One day in April, a lookout high up in the rigging shouted 'White rock ahead!' As *Investigator* drew closer, the 'white rock' turned into another ship. Was it an enemy vessel? Were they about to be attacked? Matthew immediately ordered the ship's guns to be prepared for action. He hoisted the British flag, and a white flag that signalled a request for peaceful contact.

To Matthew's surprise it was a French ship, called *Géographe*. She was one of two French expeditionary ships that had left France to explore Australia the previous October. *Investigator* and *Géographe* approached each other. Matthew launched a boat and was invited aboard the French ship. She was under the command of Captain Nicolas Baudin. Matthew showed Captain Baudin his French passport, while Captain Baudin showed Matthew his English one. Baudin was engaged in exactly the same exploration as Matthew, only from east to west – the opposite direction to *Investigator*. She had become separated from her sister ship, *Naturaliste*, in stormy weather around Van Diemen's Land. In the following two days the men pored over and discussed each other's charts and observations. In fact Baudin had already taken possession of a stretch of 900 kilometres between what is now Melbourne and Adelaide for France, calling the whole area Terre Napoleon. (At the time, the first explorer to chart a coast was the first to claim the land for his country.) The two commanders went their separate ways as respected rivals but not enemies. Matthew called their meeting point Encounter Bay.

On 9 May 1802 every man was on deck eagerly working *Investigator* into Port Jackson, 'one of the finest harbours in the world'. It was ten months since they'd left England. They were in high spirits. When they landed the Sydney people remarked that the men reminded them of England with their 'fresh colour'. They were in excellent shape. Not one seaman was on the sick list. Matthew put this down to his strict orders that 'on every fine day the deck below and the cockpits should be cleaned, washed, aired with (hot iron) stoves and sprinkled with vinegar'. Every two or three weeks he ordered that the crew's beds 'and the contents of their chests and bags were opened out and exposed to the sun and air'. To avoid scurvy, a mixture of 'lime juice and sugar' was drunk. Pickled cabbage was given to the crew when limes were not available. The men 'drank freely' from the cask of fresh water on board and they had rum rations of 250 millilitres per sailor per day. Matthew even encouraged music and dancing, and 'other playful amusements' twice a week. Perhaps Samuel, whose father had enrolled him in dance classes, led the dancing. Maybe the men sang

'What Shall We Do With the Drunken Sailor?' and other sea shanties accompanied by their fiddles, fifes and drums.

On arrival Matthew immediately went to the new governor, Philip King. He requested the refit and repair of *Investigator* and confirmed the services of *Lady Nelson*, which had been sent ahead from England to act as a support ship for the next voyage. 'I can assure you that I will be pleased to provide every assistance necessary,' King told him. He was always ready to help Matthew.

Matthew saw that *Géographe*'s sister ship, *Naturaliste*, was anchored in the port. He was eager to meet the commander, Captain Jacques Hamelin. It was a friendly encounter during which Matthew told Hamelin of his experience with Captain Baudin. As promised Matthew passed on Baudin's message that he intended to head for Sydney as soon as bad weather set in. While they were in port, news arrived of the longed-for peace between France and England. It produced a festive mood in the whole colony.

Six weeks later Captain Baudin's ship *Géographe* turned up. 'It was grievous to see the miserable condition to which both officers and crew were reduced by scurvy,' Matthew wrote. Out of the 170 men aboard, Matthew noted, only 12 were capable of work. The rest had succumbed to the dreaded scurvy and were sent straight to hospital. Governor King helped Baudin and his crew with medical attention and fresh fruit and vegetables. He organised repairs to *Géographe*. There was entertainment. Governor King invited the officers to parties, dances and dinners at Government House. In return, dinner parties were held on board the French and English ships, which Matthew found 'particularly agreeable'.

Every day, a quarter of an hour before dinner was served, Trim would be ready in the officers' dining room. He sat up on the table, perfectly quiet and well-behaved, until all the company was served their food. Then he would utter a very small 'meow' as a modest request for a little food from each plate. If he was not given it he would whip a morsel of meat off the fork between the plate and the mouth of the officer. But he didn't run off with his prize shamefaced. He sat gracefully chewing his mouthful. Trim's skill was so great that no-one could be cross with him. In fact, his dexterity and poise were admired. But it was a different matter when there were guests. On one occasion, a visitor was talking at dinner, his fork held in mid-air with a piece of mutton on the end of it. Trim, whose absolute favourite dish was mutton, quickly removed the meat before the speaker knew what had happened.

'What in the devil's name? Do you allow the cat to eat with you?' the guest asked crossly, to the amusement of the rest of the company.

'Why, certainly. He's one of our best officers,' Matthew said, to the annoyance of the guest.

Matthew took the opportunity to write letters home to Ann, his sister Elizabeth, his father and stepmother, and other family and friends. Together with copies of his charts, he put them aside to be sent to England by the next ship.

Before setting sail on *Géographe* for more exploration, Baudin left a copy of a letter with Governor King. It was addressed to the administration of Île de France (now called Mauritius), a French-held island in the Indian Ocean. He was so thankful for the hospitality he and his crew had received from Governor King that he wrote a letter of recommendation, so that a British ship landing in Île de France would be welcomed as he had been welcomed in Sydney. On the letter he left a space for the name of the ship and of the captain to be filled in. Governor King put the letter aside and forgot about it. Matthew was not to know how fortune might have blessed him instead of cursing him if King had only remembered to give him that letter.

King recommended nine convicts-for-life, mostly sailors, as extra crew for *Investigator* to take the place of the men who had died in Memory Cove. With good conduct they would be freed at the end of the voyage. Two volunteer Aboriginal men were invited on board. Matthew knew Bungaree as his 'humble friend' from trips in *Reliance* five years previously, and described him as a 'worthy and brave fellow'. He was a Kuringgai man from north of Sydney who had proved himself to be an excellent communicator with other Aboriginal peoples. Nanbaree was 'a good-natured lad' from the local Eora Aboriginal group. Bungaree and Nanbaree's roles were to 'bring about a friendly intercourse with the inhabitants of other parts of the coast'.

Trim and Bungaree soon became firm friends. Bungaree had never seen a domestic cat before. If Trim wanted to eat or drink he simply said 'mew' to Bungaree, who would give him water or some baked black swan. All the swans in Australia were black, unlike the white swans that are native to Europe. Nobody knows why. Trim loved Bungaree and often sat beside him, paying him generously with licks and rubs.

Meanwhile massive quantities of supplies were being loaded onto *Investigator*. The groaning crew and dock workers dragged up the gangplank 13,600 kilograms of bread and biscuits, 360 kilograms of flour, 1520 kilograms of dried wheat, hundreds of litres of beer and 67,400 litres of rum, together with tobacco and salted meat. Live sheep, pigs, geese and ducks were boarded for fresh meat on the 12-month journey. With every space packed, the repaired *Investigator* sailed from Port Jackson accompanied by her support ship *Lady Nelson* on 22 July 1802. How pleased Matthew must have felt to be on his way at last.

As they sailed north up the coast of New South Wales, Matthew drew detailed maps and recorded weather and sea conditions. The coast had been charted by Captain Cook, but with older, less accurate equipment. Matthew was able to correct Cook's readings, especially of latitude and longitude. Because Cook had sailed past a number of places during the night he'd missed seeing important bays, landing places and harbours. Matthew mapped these by making sure to drop the anchor at night and only sail during daylight hours.

Ten days later, while leading a landing party with Bungaree, Matthew and four crewmen were confronted by angry Aboriginal men waving sticks and gesturing at them to go back. Bungaree stripped off his European clothes. As naked as his fellow countrymen, he approached the group, speaking to them in his own language, then in broken English. They were 1000 kilometres from Sydney, and Bungaree and the local people were unable to understand each other's languages. It may have been that the locals did not want to accept foreigners on their territory without the proper introductory rituals, which would have been unknown to Flinders' party and even to Bungaree.

Eventually tempers cooled and friendly relations were established. A feast of porpoise blubber had been prepared by the crew so they could maintain good terms with the local people. Remembering how Captain Cook had been killed by natives in Hawaii over a quarrel about a missing boat in 1779, Matthew was particularly keen to ensure his safety and that of his crew. He wanted to leave good relationships in place for any Europeans who might follow in his footsteps.

A week later the botanist Robert Brown rowed ashore with six companions to explore the vegetation on Facing Island near today's town of Gladstone, 1500 kilometres north of Sydney. A group of Aboriginal men had gathered to look at the ship but ran off when the crew walked ashore. The group stood on a hill above the beach and started throwing stones at the ship's men. They were only stopped when the crew fired musket shots over their heads, whereupon the local people disappeared and stayed hidden from view. They weren't seen again.

Not long after this, Matthew, Robert Brown and a small number of crew took the rowing boat ashore with supplies to investigate the route of a river in Keppel Bay. Sleeping overnight near mangrove swamps, they were bitten alive by swarms of mosquitoes and sand flies. One enviable seaman snored through the night. Maybe his skin was not tasty enough for the biting insects to feed upon or, according to Matthew's report, they 'could not penetrate his skin'. The company, most of them irritable from lack of sleep and very itchy, pressed on, making notes about the twists and turns of the river. Having spent the night with the maddening zings of mosquitoes in their ears and scratching night and day, it was with great relief that they finished their charting and returned to the ship.

As soon as Matthew arrived on board he found

that two sailors who had gone ashore were missing. It was now dark so unlikely that they would turn up. He spent a restless, anxious night. When morning came he ordered two guns to be fired and a lieutenant was sent to search for the men. Matthew became increasingly worried, thinking about what might have happened to them on a strange shore with no compass to guide them, and unfamiliar Aboriginal groups about.

By evening the two had returned, 'ludicrous figures … their cloaths all rags without Shoes or Stockings having all Stuck in the mud', as Peter Good, the ship's gardener, wrote. They told of becoming separated from their companions and finding themselves lost in the mangrove swamps, where they spent a night attacked by clouds of mosquitoes. In the morning they woke up, startled to find that they were surrounded by Aboriginal men. The locals didn't look aggressive and directed them to their fire place, where they fed them with baked duck. Then they walked the two men back to the ship. Matthew was so relieved that he sent a boat ashore, according to Samuel Smith, one of the seamen, 'with Drum, Fife and Fiddle, likewise presents' as a display of gratitude to the local people. What the Aboriginal people thought of the strange foreigners and their music is not recorded.

Whenever the wind whistled and the sails shook it always produced a great commotion on deck. The sailors shouted, their bare feet pounding the boards. Trim would dash upstairs just in time to hear the cry 'Away up aloft!' In a flash, Trim would run up the rigging faster than any sailor. He sat on a small shelf on the mainmast – called the cap, or crow's nest – with his golden eyes gazing down at the hard-working crew. They stretched themselves out on the yard arms, which held the flapping sails, hauling in the heavy canvas with their calloused hands. The sailors were not at all jealous when Trim assumed such a position of superiority. One of them would always stroke him after the job was done and carry him down the rope ladder tucked under one arm.

All the time *Lady Nelson*, a smaller, slower ship, had repeatedly fallen behind, either making *Investigator* wait, or by agreement meeting at a pre-arranged place later in the day. Now *Lady Nelson*, steering too close to the coast, struck a reef and lost part of her keel (underneath the ship). She was still seaworthy but no longer so useful for sailing in shallow waters, which was one of the main reasons she had accompanied

Investigator. A safe harbour was found with fresh water. This allowed the carpenters to find wood to build and attach a new keel. It took them a week to finish the job.

In early August one of *Lady Nelson*'s anchors, which had snagged on a rock, broke when it was lifted up. Another was lost in the sea when the ship swung in a violent tide rushing between two reefs. The captain, John Murray, asked Matthew for a spare anchor. Matthew couldn't give him one because his own needed repair. He was only able to provide a light pronged anchor – called a grapnel. Both ships were now short of strong anchors, which were needed to hold the ships securely when they stopped for the night. Two months later, in the middle of the night, *Investigator* dragged her anchor for several kilometres. Neither of the men on watch had noticed. From the log it looked as though Matthew's brother Samuel was responsible for the blunder, but Matthew decided to leave the matter, unless something like it was to happen a second time. It had been a serious error. If the ship had swung onto rocks it could have been smashed to splinters and all the men drowned.

By September the men were tired. They had no fresh food and were getting little sleep, having to reset the sails every time the wind speed or direction changed, whether night or day. The small sailing cutter, their emergency boat, had been lost when it was hauled up in a fast-running tide, filled with water and swept away. The boatman was thrown into the sea but was rescued by *Lady Nelson*'s boat. There was drunkenness, a fight broke out, the boatswain was suspended from duty and a seaman was given 12 lashes of the whip for striking an officer. Matthew was feeling too exhausted to go ashore, so he took survey readings from the ship. Second Lieutenant Samuel Flinders, Matthew's brother, was responsible for winding up the sea clocks, which were essential for measuring longitude. Matthew became irritated with Samuel when he repeatedly let the clocks wind down and stop. He grumbled at him and reminded Samuel of his duties. He wrote to Ann that Samuel was as 'inferior to other officers as I would have him superior'. Tensions were developing between the bossy older commander-brother and the lower-ranking brother who was eight years younger.

One day *Lady Nelson* caught on a bank of quicksand and became stuck. While she floated off at high tide, the copper bottoms, which covered her keel to protect it from barnacles, seaweed and rot, were wrenched off.

She could still sail, but without the special covering underneath the ship to prevent attack by shipworm and weeds that would eat into the timbers.

Both ships had spent a month attempting to navigate and chart the maze of dangerous shoals, reefs, sandbanks and coral islets along the north-east coast of Australia. *Lady Nelson*, still trying to sail in the shallowest water, kept running aground in the sand. Matthew was faced with impossibly detailed and difficult charting. They were caught up in the treacherous Great Barrier Reef where Captain Cook's ship, *Endeavour*, had narrowly escaped being wrecked in 1770. Matthew agonised over his options.

～ Six ～

Despite the tremendous challenges, Matthew drove *Investigator* on towards Torres Strait in the extreme north. The monsoon season threatened and they would soon be caught in torrential rain and electrical storms. He didn't know that ferocious cyclones also struck the northern coast at this time of year. Neither did Matthew have any idea of the length of the Great Barrier Reef, which still lay in the ship's path and formed a coral obstacle course more than 2000 kilometres long. Breakers crashed up against the seaward side of the reef, throwing up high foamy columns of spray and giving the impression that it was impassable. However, with stubbornness and willpower Matthew threaded his ship through the network of reefs until October. By then *Investigator* had lost one of her last two anchors in a rushing torrent between the reefs. *Lady Nelson* not only had two patched anchors but a damaged hull. She leaned to one side as she sailed. Matthew was worried that she was at risk of going down. Rather than *Lady Nelson* supporting *Investigator* it looked like *Investigator* would be forced to rescue *Lady Nelson*. Matthew restlessly chewed over what he should do.

The next day Matthew came to the difficult decision to send *Lady Nelson* back to Port Jackson alone. He wrote that he regretted 'parting from our little consort' but the expedition needed to do much more surveying before monsoons hit the coast. The young Aboriginal man, Nanbaree, longing to return to his tribe in Sydney, boarded *Lady Nelson* for the journey home. Matthew was glad to at least be able to send letters to Ann and his family with Captain Murray. On the morning of 18 October they 'showed their colours', raising their flags as a farewell salute.

The crews waved each other off, and *Lady Nelson* steered south while *Investigator* sailed on northward. Matthew, looking to the task ahead, had only a few imperfect maps by previous explorers to guide him.

Like someone learning to weave a thread backwards and forwards row by row, Matthew patiently charted between the Great Barrier Reef and the shoreline. Anxiously watching every ripple of the sea for hidden coral and rocks, he travelled in the calmer inner waters for 14 days. When he was uncertain of *Investigator*'s ability to 'thread the needle', he climbed into a rowing boat to check the sea depth and bottom, or mounted an island hill to look ahead of him.

After sailing 800 kilometres in the Great Barrier Reef he finally found a safe channel between the reefs out to the open sea, a route that is now called Flinders Passage. It was this much-needed escape route out of the path of the hazardous coral islands that allowed him to sail up to Cape York and round into the Gulf of Carpentaria. However, by the end of October *Investigator* was starting to take on water to a worrying degree, 'at ten inches per hour' (25 centimetres). Matthew ordered the carpenters to make a complete survey of the ship's timbers.

He must have sat down heavily and gasped with

alarm when he read the report. Many of the timbers were found to be rotten through. Nails and fixings were rusted and loose. The carpenters' conclusion was that in fair weather the ship might last six months, but in 'unfavourable circumstances, she would immediately go to pieces' and sink.

Matthew was appalled by the news. He could see his dreams evaporating, his name as a world-class explorer fading, and the possibilities of promotion and wealth disappearing. The last thing he wanted to do was to return to Port Jackson. It would mean abandoning his exploration of the Gulf of Carpentaria, which would not only be against the Admiralty's orders but contrary to his own passionate desires. Besides, to turn back would involve sailing directly into the monsoon winds in a ship that 'would hardly escape foundering' – sinking. It was far too dangerous. He wrote that he wanted his charting to be so complete and accurate that 'no navigator (need) come after me'. In fact his charts were so exquisitely exact they were used for 140 years. His chart of the Great Australian Bight has never been repeated. After agonising over his course of action he made up his mind: he would continue charting until the monsoon season ended in April 1803, then return to Port Jackson.

At the end of 1802 Matthew zigzagged *Investigator* through the confusing scatter of islands in the narrow Torres Strait at the northern tip of Australia, just south of New Guinea. Although two or three earlier explorers had sailed through the dangerous Strait, Matthew's meticulous map was a huge breakthrough in navigation. It would save as much as five or six weeks for a journey between the Pacific and the Indian Oceans where previously, to be safe, ships passed north of New Guinea, travelling an extra 2000 kilometres. Matthew's chart was the most detailed and the most reliable.

Early in the new year, when the ship was well into the Gulf of Carpentaria, the whaleboat, an open boat pointed at both ends, was launched to check the depth of the uneven sea bottom ahead of *Investigator*. For a moment the whaleboat was forced towards the ship. It veered to avoid a collision, but suddenly filled with water and the two men in it, William Job and William Murray, were thrown into the sea and disappeared. Matthew immediately launched another boat to rescue them. William Job reappeared unharmed and was pulled aboard, but William Murray, who couldn't swim, never surfaced and was lost. The whaleboat was severely damaged.

Three weeks later a firewood, fishing and botanical party went ashore and, noticing a group of six Aboriginal men who had arrived by canoe, went to meet them. The men advanced holding their spears at the ready. The crew and marines gripped their muskets. Matthew wrote in his journal that Thomas Whitewood, the master's mate, 'who was foremost, put out his hand to receive a spear which he supposed was offered; but (one of the Aboriginal men), thinking perhaps that an attempt was made to take his arms, ran the spear into the breast of his supposed enemy'. Matthew heard gunshots from the ship and immediately dispatched two armed boats under the command of the master, John Aken. He ordered Aken to be friendly to the Aboriginal men, but warned that if he found that the locals had been the aggressors Aken should confiscate their canoe.

Instead of following these orders, Aken's party gave chase and shot one of the Aboriginal men. When Matthew learned about the incident he was 'much concerned' and 'greatly displeased'. He assumed from his knowledge of the timid nature of many Aboriginal people that the aggression must have originated from his crew. His orders had been not to chase after the locals. He was annoyed that his command had been disobeyed but felt there was nothing more he could do.

On the same day one of the marines, who had worn no hat in the burning sun all day, suffered severe heatstroke and died of convulsions (fits) that evening. Thomas Whitewood's spear wounds were cleaned and bandaged by Hugh Bell and he slowly recovered.

At the time the risk of death was very high, not only to seafarers. There was just a tiny number of effective medicines, no anaesthetics, and operations were not performed in clean conditions. Most people had a very poor diet, and many had unhealthy living conditions. Everyone, at least on land, had to pay the doctor or go without any medical care at all.

Matthew continued his survey in northern Australia. He followed and corrected a chart of the Gulf of Carpentaria completed in 1644 by the explorer Abel Tasman. Explorers from all the European countries shared copies of each other's maps, even when their countries were at war with each other.

In February 1803, after being shaken and soaked by the monsoon storms, squalls, heavy rains, thunder and lightning, the ship rounded Cape Arnhem on the western side of the Gulf of Carpentaria. They came upon a string of islands that were so close together it was difficult to see the openings between them. *Investigator* had just passed through a narrow passage when the officers on watch suddenly saw a large canoe full of men, alongside six covered boats, tucked in close to a rocky island. Looking straight ahead, Matthew could not see a way out at the other end of the stretch of water. Was it a trap? What were the men doing there? Were they going to ambush the ship? 'Pirates!' thought Matthew. He immediately hoisted the British flag and the white ensign of peace. He waited.

Soon he saw the foreigners hoist their white flags. Matthew sent his brother Samuel in an armed boat to find out who the men were. Why not send an annoying younger brother into a tricky situation? Every eye was on the two boats as they advanced. They were within musket shot of each other. They drew closer. The meeting was peaceful. Then six commanders returned with Samuel and boarded *Investigator*. Each man wore a short dagger by his side so Matthew's men kept a hold of their guns.

The visitors were Malays from Macassar in

Indonesia. Fortunately Matthew's cook, Abraham Williams, was Malay so he could speak their language. The chief, Pobassoo, was a short, elderly man. Abraham talked to Pobassoo and found out about his business. The Malays had brought 60 boats with 1000 men and travelled 2000 kilometres from Macassar. The area around Bromby's Isles attracted them because of the abundance of sea cucumbers there. In China, these creatures were prized as a medicine and health food. The Malays had been visiting the islands and trading sea cucumber with the Chinese for 20 years. Pobassoo was on his seventh voyage and had never seen another ship. In fact the trade had very likely been going on for hundreds of years and was well known to the Aboriginal communities along the northern coast of Australia. As Muslims, the Malays were horrified at the sight of live pigs being kept on board *Investigator*, but were delighted by Trim's tricks and friendly approaches. The officers opened a bottle of port wine, which the visitors enjoyed so much they took another one away with them.

By March, Hugh Bell, the ship's surgeon, was becoming increasingly worried about the health of the exhausted men. He urged Matthew to head back to Port Jackson without delay, itself a journey of three months. The wind had moved to the east, and the worst of the rain and storms had ceased, marking an end to the monsoon season. But it was ideal weather for Matthew to survey the next stretch of coast round to the west. Matthew dug his heels in. He wanted to chart as much as he could before returning, even though he himself was now suffering from crippling foot ulcers caused by scurvy. The ulcers – painful weeping sores – stopped him from going ashore, as his feet hurt too much to get in and out of a rowing boat. Hugh Bell, growing more and more uneasy about the men's health, nagged Matthew to leave. They disagreed and their relationship turned irritable and argumentative. In the end Matthew asked Bell to provide a full medical report on all the crew.

The report showed that 22 men were suffering from scurvy. Five men were too ill to work. They lay in their hammocks all day, moaning with pain, unable to eat because of their dry, sore mouths. All the crew were suffering from fatigue. Bell prescribed a course of lime juice, which was rich in vitamin C. However, when the cases of juice were brought up from the ship's hold, Bell must have despaired to see that many of the bottles had smashed with the ship's movement. The remainder Matthew insisted on keeping for the next voyage around the west coast, which, he wrote, 'would probably be much longer.' How Hugh Bell must have fumed. For three months there had been recurrent diarrhoea going around the crew, which Bell thought was due to the hot, wet weather. Diarrhoea is a symptom of scurvy, and it was further weakening the men. Even the stench must have made the men's stomachs churn. By now Matthew, just 29 years old, found his hair was turning grey; so was Trim's. Matthew had lost weight; Trim had lost all his claws and spent more and more time sleeping.

The ship's stores of peas, rice and sugar were critically low. Matthew, feeling beaten down, was beginning to realise with dismay that he 'may never again return to accomplish' his goal. Reluctantly he forced himself to abandon charting and set the sails for the return journey to Port Jackson. First he directed *Investigator* to Kupang, a Dutch port on the island of Timor 1300 kilometres away, to restock food and water. There was nowhere nearer. Matthew sat down with Robert Fowler, the second-in-command, and agreed a plan to send him back to England on the next ship from Kupang. Fowler's instructions were to ask the Admiralty for another ship to finish charting the remaining coast. Ten days before they arrived in Kupang a British ship from India had already left for England and no-one knew when another would arrive. Matthew's plans were again thwarted. Fowler stayed on board. Matthew must have wondered whether fortune would ever shine on him again.

Fresh fruit and vegetables, rice, meat, provisions for the animals and water were bought and loaded. But there was no salt available, something that was essential in the hot tropical climate to replace salt the men lost by sweating. This finally convinced Matthew that he couldn't possibly continue his explorations. He wrote letters reporting his findings to the Admiralty, and personal letters to Ann, other family members and friends. His letters were given to the captain of a Dutch vessel that was leaving for Indonesia, to be sent on from there with the next ship to England.

For a week *Investigator* underwent urgent repairs. The weary men were allowed shore leave every day when their work was done, but after a few days Matthew's cook, Abraham Williams, and a young man from Port Jackson did not return. Had they become lost, or worse? Had they run away? Two searches were made in the town without success. With great disappointment Matthew realised that *Investigator* had to leave the two deserters behind.

Sailing from Timor, Matthew remained determined to seize every opportunity, so he squeezed in one last chance to explore. The Admiralty had asked him to check an area called Trial Rocks, named after an English ship, *Trial*, that had been wrecked there in 1622. The Rocks were recorded on different maps in different places. Matthew spent five days sailing backwards and forwards unable to find anything that resembled Trial Rocks. Only then did he head back to Port Jackson.

The sky was the colour of lead, with black clouds meeting a choppy, metal-grey sea. Drenching downpours hit the ship to a background of thunder and lightning. Ten men were off sick with diarrhoea and fever. The only treatment the surgeon could give was to soak the patients in warm sea water. Diarrhoea spread to others in the crowded seamen's quarters. Their hammocks strung from the ceiling beams were barely

12 centimetres apart. The men's diarrhoea worsened over the next month, despite frequent cleaning of the areas with hot water and vinegar. Imagine the stink. The toilet was a hole in a wooden board with the sea underneath. No toilet paper; maybe some rags. No hand basin to wash in, not even sea water in a bucket. The idea of handwashing didn't exist then. No wonder the illness spread so dangerously from sailor to sailor.

The first man to die from dysentery, a deadly and highly contagious bowel infection, was the boatswain, Charles Douglas. Matthew blamed it on the water they had taken on board in Kupang, but where could he obtain fresh supplies? There was no other port. Three days later William Hillier, the quartermaster, died. We can only imagine Matthew's feelings of despair, simply writing in his journal that Hillier was 'one of my best men'. After a week James Greenhalgh, the sergeant of the marines, died too. Ten days later the new quartermaster, John Draper, was dead, and 18 men were sick, 'stretched in their hammocks almost without hope'. When a man died, his body was sewn into his hammock. Matthew would recite a short funeral service, then the body would be 'committed to the deep' – slid down a plank into the sea. Later the men's belongings would be sold to the other sailors.

Matthew resolved to get back to Port Jackson as soon as he could, although all the while 'making such observations ... as could be done without causing delay'. He never gave up. As soon as *Investigator* docked in Sydney on 9 June 1803, Matthew hurried to Governor King to arrange for the sick to be transferred to the colonial hospital. Thomas Smith, one of the ex-convicts, had died a few hours before arriving in Sydney, and four more men died over the following few days.

~ Seven ~

More heavy blows awaited Matthew in Port Jackson. He received a letter from his stepmother informing him that his father had died, aged 51. Matthew was stunned. He had planned to make his father's final years 'the most delightful of his life'. He was full of remorse that he couldn't now let his father know how much he loved him. His inability to help his family so far away filled him with regret and a yearning to be home. To give them and himself hope he wrote back that 'at this time I consider our business to be nearly half done; therefore, as we left England in July 1801, we ought to arrive again about the same time in 1805'. It seemed a reasonable enough calculation. But life was not going to treat Matthew reasonably.

The ulcers on his feet finally healed due to his fresh vegetable diet in Sydney. How overjoyed he was then to receive six letters from Ann. When they had parted she had been so upset about being abruptly separated that she didn't write to him at all. Now she was catching up. Matthew wrote back: 'my mind retraces with delight, our joys … our everything of love'.

Trim's health also improved on a diet of fresh meat. His coat was now glossy black again, and he started to put on weight. When Matthew weighed him, the scale read 14 pounds (6.4 kilograms). Trim was the weight of two newborn babies. Matthew described him as 'fat and frisky' and was glad of his warmth as 'a bedfellow' in the cold, rainy Sydney winter.

He was impatient to plan the final mapping of the uncharted western coast of Australia. However, there was no suitable ship available in Port Jackson, and *Investigator* was so rotten she could only be used as a hulk – a stationary prison ship. He decided to return to England to request another ship from the Admiralty.

In Port Jackson there was a better ship, HMS *Porpoise*, which was almost the same size as *Investigator*. She was occupied collecting and delivering supplies for the colonies of Sydney and Norfolk Island, but eventually she was made ready to take Matthew and Trim back to England as passengers. Single-minded Matthew insisted on returning via Torres Strait, to perfect the charting of that coastline and its many islands before leaving Australian waters. Trim was carried on board and soon found a 'comfortable niche' in Matthew's cabin.

On 10 August 1803 the *Porpoise* sailed from Port Jackson in the company of two other ships – *Cato* and *Bridgewater*, both on their way to Batavia (now Jakarta) in Indonesia. Their captains were keen to experience first-hand the new shorter and surer way through Torres Strait that would lead them directly to Indonesia. Matthew took great pride in showing them his map of the route he had charted nine months before.

A week after the three ships left, they were sailing along what is now the Queensland coast, 80 kilometres from the shore. It was a black night with no moon. Did Matthew hear waves breaking or was it the wind in the flapping sails? Suddenly he heard scraping, a screech and a terrible crash. He was thrown across the gun room where he had been talking with other officers. The ship lurched onto her side. Water poured across the decks. *Porpoise* had struck a coral reef.

The men stood silently on deck, horrified, staring out. *Cato* and *Bridgewater* had followed *Porpoise*. They'd heard the crash and changed direction to avoid smashing into *Porpoise*. But they were heading straight for each other. The men on *Porpoise* held their breath. All eyes strained to see what would happen. Then 'they set up a great shout to warn the ships'. At the last minute the two ships veered away from each other just enough to avoid colliding. In doing so *Cato* hit the reef, rolled over and disappeared. *Bridgewater* passed by further out, escaped the reef and, from the light on her mast, could be seen sailing straight on.

Porpoise was stuck on top of the reef. Huge waves lifted and dropped her with such force that the mainmast broke away. It fell with an almighty bang. The keel was smashed in. Captain Aken ordered the other two masts to be thrown overboard and the anchor to be cut away. By lightening the ship he hoped it could be washed further up onto the reef and held fast, so avoiding being washed away under the waves.

Matthew decided to take his precious logs and journals, the only proof of his painstaking charting, out to *Bridgewater* for safe-keeping. He expected to be able to guide *Bridgewater* back to the rescue. He jumped into the water and swam to one of the rowing boats that had already been launched. How he kept his journals dry is not known. The rowing boat already held six sailors. There was nothing in it to bail out water, and two odd oars. It soon became obvious that in the dark, with the waves crashing onto the reef, no-one from *Bridgewater* could possibly have rescued the shipwrecked men that night.

Matthew and the men stayed in the boat overnight, bailing out the water with their shoes. The salty spray soaked their clothes and a fresh breeze made them shiver. The men were waiting to alert *Bridgewater* at sunrise. Several blue oil lamps were burned to attract her attention, but at 2 o'clock in the morning *Bridgewater*'s own light could no longer be seen. In the meantime, Matthew and the men stayed as close as they could to *Porpoise* in case she broke up. They could at least rescue some of her crew.

At daylight *Bridgewater*'s sails were visible on the horizon but she was sailing away from them. Soon she was out of sight. Matthew and the seamen, feeling wretched and chilled to the bone, returned to *Porpoise*. There was bitter criticism of Captain Palmer, *Bridgewater*'s master, for not coming back to help them. Matthew felt abandoned.

A year later Matthew was sickened to read Captain Palmer's report in which he stated that both ships had sunk with no survivors. Palmer wrote that *Bridgewater* was unable to get anywhere near *Cato* and *Porpoise* because of the breakers crashing onto the reef. It was obvious that Palmer had not even tried to return to the wrecks to see what could be done. Matthew could only imagine what Captain Palmer's thoughts must have been when his own ship, *Bridgewater*, was lost at sea later that year. She and Captain Palmer were never found.

Cato had capsized partly under the water, partly onto the reef. The force of the pounding waves had practically broken up the ship. Men were clinging to pieces of wreckage. Others were in the water. One 'poor boy' had been shipwrecked on each of his three voyages and survived. This time he 'bewailed himself through the night', then lost his grip on a broken sail pole and 'was not seen afterwards'. Two of the other boys from *Cato* also drowned.

The men on *Cato* huddled together, terrified, on the front of the ship, the only part that was completely out of the water. They were shouting: 'Help! Help!' Matthew sent a rowing boat to them numerous times to bring as many men as possible back to *Porpoise* for shelter, food and clothing.

Standing on deck with his telescope, Matthew scanned the area. Imagine the thrill he must have felt when he spied a large sandbank less than a kilometre away. He and the captain's mate, Robert Fowler, took a small two-masted brig (a sailing boat) over to inspect it. They were immensely relieved to find that the bank was more than 2 kilometres long and over a kilometre wide. Judging by the birds' nests on it, it was obviously above the waterline and fit to be made into a camp.

They returned with the good news. Matthew remembered that when Robinson Crusoe had been washed up on a desert island, he swam to the wreckage of his ship, made a raft from broken wood and took everything he could use back to dry land.

Now everybody's job was to shift all the unspoiled cargo, the surviving sheep and pigs, and the men from both ships to their temporary home on the sandbank. It took five days to move everything that could be used. Tents were made from *Porpoise*'s sails. Even the armourer's forge had been saved – the iron block on which weapons were made and repaired. Trim was carried over in a sailor's arms and set down to guard the bread. He immediately pounced upon the mice that had come ashore with the cargo. Matthew wrote that he always took his duties very seriously. Trim must have appreciated his morsels of fresh meat when the journey had taken such a terrible turn.

The 80 men made themselves as comfortable as they could, divided into tents by rank. They had enough food and water, including wine and spirits, for three months. On the highest part of the bank they raised a flag in case *Bridgewater* returned to look for them.

Although Matthew was not the ship's commander, he was experienced enough to take charge. He called a meeting of all the officers. They agreed that he and John Murray, the captain of *Cato*, would take one of the brigs, which they named *Hope*, with 12 crewmen. They would head for Port Jackson as fast as they could to ask to be rescued. Matthew gave orders that if they weren't back after six weeks, some of the remaining crew should set out for Port Jackson themselves in two rowing boats.

It took Matthew and the men in *Hope* two weeks to row and sail day and night in the open boat to cover the 1200 kilometres to Port Jackson. This was itself an amazing achievement. With enormous relief Matthew steered the boat into the calm waters of Sydney Harbour. He thought not only of the men waiting to be rescued on the sandbank, but of his charts and journals for which he'd worked so hard.

When the governor of New South Wales, Philip King, set eyes on the men he was astonished. It was not only that they were back in Sydney instead of being on their way to England, but they were scruffy and smelly, and had grown untidy beards. King was horrified when he heard about the shipwreck: 'an involuntary tear started from the (governor's) eye of friendship and compassion', Matthew wrote.

Without delay King ordered three ships to be made ready for the rescue. One would bring back sailors who wanted to return to Sydney. Another would travel on to England, stopping first in China. The third, *Cumberland*, was a tiny ship of 29 tons that had been built in Sydney two years previously for local use. She was one-tenth the size of *Porpoise*.

On 7 October the three ships arrived at the sandbank, exactly six weeks after Matthew and his shipmates had left on their mercy mission. As the ships anchored that afternoon there was enormous excitement from the men on the bank. Eleven guns were fired and three cheers roared out. Matthew, delighted, wrote that his happiness 'could not be described'. The sandbank is now part of an area called Wreck Reefs, and is still there today.

Matthew decided to lose no more time and sail straight to England in the tiny *Cumberland*, finishing charting Torres Strait on the way. He wasn't giving up. His brother Samuel went home on the ship bound for England via China. Trim would not leave Matthew's side, 'a memorable example of faithful attachment', so they both set off in *Cumberland* with ten men.

It wasn't long before Matthew regretted his choice. He was disgusted to find that *Cumberland* was infested with 'bugs, lice, fleas, weavels, mosquitoes, cockroaches and mice'. Not only that, but the lightweight ship was so tossed about by the sea that Matthew could hardly write clearly in his journal. In addition, because it was so small *Cumberland* needed to keep stopping at different ports to stock up with fresh food and water.

~ Eight ~

'Land ahoy!' shouted the officer on watch. Through his telescope Matthew made out the green, mountainous outline of the French-held island, Île de France (now known as Mauritius). But where should he moor? With no chart and only a description in the *Encyclopaedia Britannica* to go by, Matthew couldn't work out where the main port was. Hesitating, he eventually guided *Cumberland* into the nearest sheltered bay, Baie du Cap. This caused lookouts on the coast to be suspicious about the purpose of this foreign ship's movements. Today, a monument to Matthew and Trim stands on the headland there.

At that time, the only way to contact someone far away was by letter. It took so many months for sailing ships to cross the world that, when people received news, it was no longer new. So Matthew had not the slightest idea that when *Cumberland* dropped anchor, France and England had been at war again for seven months. All he knew was that *Cumberland* was leaking badly, and that its wooden planks and bilge pumps needed urgent repairs. Matthew and two other crewmen were also suffering from frequent fevers, probably due to malaria caught from mosquitoes in Timor.

As Matthew stepped ashore in his salt-encrusted uniform, he was astounded to be questioned by the local army major, then the district commandant, and finally by the governor of the island, General Charles Decaen. Decaen was a passionate supporter of the Emperor Napoleon and, having worked in intelligence, was determined to combat any threat to the security of Île de France. The general didn't believe that Matthew could really be an official British explorer if he had sailed all the way from Australia in a ship no bigger than a river ferry. All three officials were suspicious of the French passport Matthew held, which he had waited so long for in England and now utterly depended upon. It referred to his ship as *Investigator*, not *Cumberland*. Matthew explained that he had been forced to abandon *Investigator* and had been shipwrecked in *Porpoise*, but Decaen decided it was just a tall tale to get Matthew out of trouble. His interrogators felt their suspicions had been confirmed when Matthew denied any knowledge of the famous navigator 'Monsieur Flinedare', which he only later realised was his own name. Decaen angrily accused Matthew of being an English spy.

His passport was taken away along with his treasured logbooks and charts, and all his private papers. Matthew was furious about Decaen's unreasonable behaviour. He believed Decaen must soon realise his mistake and told himself that it would only be a matter of days before he was released. He underlined his case by immediately writing to Decaen, outlining his arguments against his captivity.

If only he'd had with him the letter left by Captain Nicolas Baudin with Governor King in Sydney that recommended the British to the French. In fact Baudin himself had been living on Île de France that year but had died of tuberculosis three months before Matthew arrived. *Géographe*, Baudin's ship, had left Île de France just the day before *Cumberland* anchored in the harbour. This was another knock to add to the list of rotten luck that had hit Matthew and the crew.

Matthew, along with *Cumberland*'s captain John Aken, their two servants and Trim were taken prisoner and sent to a small room in a shabby inn called Café Marengo, where they were kept under guard. It was hot, and they were plagued by mosquitoes and bedbugs.

'What! I am to be prisoner here? It is absolutely intolerable!' complained Matthew, pacing up and down. He felt miserable, hot, sweaty and very itchy. The bad diet caused Matthew's foot sores to break out again. Fluid oozed down his feet and the smell was foul. He asked to see the surgeon, who cleaned and bandaged them, and ordered him fresh fruit and vegetables. It didn't help his case to be freed when, in the first few days, Matthew snubbed General Decaen by refusing his invitation to dinner, stating furiously: 'Only when I should be set at liberty!'

Trim meowed and scratched at the door. He didn't like being imprisoned in the small room any more than the men did. Every day he would sneak past the guard at the door to explore the neighbourhood. He returned later and later each night, until one evening Matthew decided it was safer to shut Trim indoors after supper.

All the time Matthew was trying to obtain his release by repeatedly writing to General Decaen, explaining his case in great detail and pleading his innocence. He felt insulted not to receive a single reply. He was allowed to write letters home but they had to be opened and read by a censor, who checked and crossed out the wording if it was not approved.

Eight weeks later, Jacques Bergeret, a French sea captain who'd been treated well by the British as a prisoner of war, arrived on Île de France. Hearing about Matthew's troubles he decided to pay him a visit, captain to captain. Taking pity on him, Bergeret went to see General Decaen. He managed to arrange for Matthew, John Aken, their servants and Trim to be moved to a large government building 2 kilometres away. It was called Maison Despeaux and housed high-ranking British prisoners of war.

Matthew felt affronted at having to pay 11 Spanish

dollars per month (about £160 today) as rent – 'perhaps the first instance of men being charged for the accommodation of a prison'. Yet he loved the clean air and fresh food in Maison Despeaux, which he called the 'Garden Prison'. After two months in the tiny *Cumberland* and another two months in the cramped, grubby Café Marengo, what a relief it was to have a large garden to exercise in. His health and strength improved and his foot ulcers at last started to heal. Matthew was pleased to at least have the opportunity to make friends with other officers. He was even allowed visitors from the outside.

After many appeals to General Decaen, most of his logs, books and private papers were finally returned, except for his last logbook. He could set to work refining and copying his charts. Despite living in greater comfort, Matthew was knocked sideways when he asked Joseph Bonnefoy, his official interpreter, how long he would be held. Bonnefoy replied, 'Until the end of the war.' The war had already lasted for a year with no end in sight. Matthew knew that wars didn't end quickly.

Trim, struggling to adjust to his life on land, would go exploring at every opportunity. Matthew, already suspicious of the authorities, feared that the guards who paid Trim a lot of attention might be plotting to capture him. A French acquaintance asked Matthew if she could keep Trim as a pet for her daughter. Matthew decided that it would be by far the safest option. The little girl loved Trim straight away.

To Matthew's horror, hardly two weeks passed before a notice was put in the local newspaper announcing Trim's disappearance. There was a reward of 10 Spanish dollars for his return (£150 today). Matthew would gladly have given five times that amount 'to have my friend and companion restored to me'. But all the searches for Trim and offers of rewards were in vain. Trim was gone. He never returned.

Matthew mourned his pet, writing: 'My sorrow may be better conceived than described … Thus perished my faithful intelligent Trim! Never, my Trim … shall I see thy like again.' During his time on Île de France he wrote his *Biographical Tribute to the Memory of Trim*, an affectionate account of Trim's character and antics. Matthew also made himself a promise: when he got back to England, to 'a thatched cottage by half an acre of land', he would raise a monument to the memory of his dearly loved cat.

While he was in captivity Matthew managed to smuggle some letters out, secretly giving them to a few chosen visitors. He wrote to the Admiralty, Sir Joseph Banks, Governor King, and Charles Fleurieu, a French navigator and Minister of the Navy. He pleaded with them to right the wrong, and arrange for him to be set free. The Admiralty wrote to the French government, and Sir Joseph Banks, president of the Royal Society (for the advancement of science), wrote to the president of the French National Institute (for the advancement of knowledge), but nothing seemed to make the slightest difference.

It was now 1805. Matthew had been captive for over 12 months. Other British prisoners had been allowed to leave the island. French prisoners of war were exchanged for British prisoners, who sailed home to England. Some prisoners escaped, stealing a boat to row out to a British ship, which rescued them. But Matthew remained.

Matthew started to suffer from excruciating back and stomach pains, and passed stones and gravel in his urine in agony. It was not the first time. After drinking a lot of weak tea, Matthew was relieved to find the pain easing after a few days.

An English-speaking local man, Thomas Pitot,

befriended Matthew. Pitot was the secretary of the Île de France Arts and Sciences' Society. He warmed to Matthew, whom he saw as an important man of science. Matthew described him as 'a young French merchant; a man well-informed, a friend to letters, to science and to the arts'. Pitot sent off letters to all the notable French men he could think of. They included the famous navigator Louis Bougainville, who had circumnavigated the globe in 1763; a councillor of the French state; a famous astronomer; and the Minister of the French Interior. Pitot argued Matthew's case for release and Matthew developed an affection for Pitot. He described his 'worthy friend' as the 'most agreeable, most useful, and at the same time durable' man. They formed a close and lasting friendship. It was one of a number of friendships Matthew made while he was in the Garden Prison. These friends were especially dear to him now that Trim was gone. More importantly, he hoped they could help him gain his freedom. In return Matthew helped Thomas Pitot obtain the release of two of his relatives held in India.

More British prisoners, including *Cumberland*'s captain John Aken, were allowed to leave on American ships sailing to England. Aken took letters and copies of Matthew's charts with him. Matthew wrote to

Decaen again, now boldly asking to be sent to France to be tried there before a court. Once more there was no reply.

Thomas Pitot managed to persuade Decaen to let Matthew and his servant, John Elder, move out of the Garden Prison. This time they went to a plantation in Wilhems Plains owned by an army widow, Madame Louise D'Arifat. She generously invited Matthew to live in the large family house on the estate. 'I had the happiness to enumerate amongst my friends one of the most worthy families in the island,' he wrote. Here Matthew enjoyed even greater freedom. He was able to mix with people within about 10 kilometres of the estate. 'I rise every morning with the sun and … bathe in the river,' he wrote. Afterwards he would 'accompany the ladies in a walk round the plantation (until) half past seven', then, after breakfast 'read and write for two hours'.

In October 1805, Matthew felt thrilled to receive a packet containing the first letters he'd had in three years from Ann and his family and friends at home. There was even an encouraging letter from Sir Joseph Banks, stating that he was doing everything he could to try to free Matthew. At Wilhems Plains Matthew had the added pleasure of taking meals with the D'Arifat family, teaching one of their daughters English and two of their sons mathematics, learning French, playing the flute, singing and playing cards. He spent time writing in his journal and copying his maps.

Recognising with a heavy heart that he was still not going to be released any time soon, Matthew and Ann devised an exciting plan. Ann suggested that she travel to Île de France to join Matthew. Pitot organised a $300 letter of credit to be sent to Matthew's London agent for her voyage. This time General Decaen sent a reply to Matthew's request. He spelled out the terms: 'Mrs Flinders should apply to the ministers of His Britannic Majesty, who should make the request to those of His Majesty the Emperor (of France).' Ann would also have needed a man to accompany her to protect her on the journey. She would have had to find a ship to America in the first instance, before changing ships and sailing on to Île de France. Decaen had put so many obstacles in her way that he had made the plan impossible to achieve. Frustrated and unhappy, the couple dropped the idea.

In 1806 Matthew managed to obtain a copy of Steel's Royal Navy List, a monthly paper which provided information about all British naval ships and their crew. He was appalled to learn that the leaking *Investigator* had actually been fully repaired in Sydney and had sailed to England the previous year. It was his ship! Surely *Investigator* would have been brought to Île de France to collect him. But no. He had heard nothing of *Investigator* when she passed Île de France, while for him another frustrating year crawled by.

Matthew was feeling more and more disheartened and low. 'There is a weight of sadness at the bottom of my heart,' he wrote. It was three years since he'd been arrested. He couldn't understand why he had not been freed. He sent more letters to distinguished men in England, increasing the number of people who knew about his cause. Time passed maddeningly slowly. That year Matthew had his portrait painted. He gazes out from the painting with blue-grey eyes set in a suntanned face, framed by dark curly hair. His lips are pressed together in determination.

Without Matthew knowing about it, there was progress toward his release. The French Emperor Napoleon had signed an order on 11 March 1806 demanding he be set free. Three copies were made and sent to Île de France on three different French ships. Two of the ships were stopped by British warships and the letters were thrown into the sea. This was the usual practice during war time. The third copy was sent to England. When the Admiralty received it they ordered it to be carried immediately to Île de France on a British warship under the white flag of peace.

By 1807 all of Matthew's crew had been set free and gone home. John Elder, Matthew's servant who refused to abandon him, had had a mental breakdown. He had been admitted to hospital where he'd remained for several weeks. When he was better, Matthew arranged for him to go home on an American ship as a member of the crew. John Elder took Matthew's letters, charts, logs and gifts in a big wooden trunk. After a journey of six months he delivered the trunk to Matthew's agent in London. When John Elder wrote to Ann, he remarked that Matthew's hair was now 'quite white'.

On 20 July 1807, an order arrived on the British warship *Greyhound* with a copy of Emperor Napoleon's document directing Decaen to release Matthew immediately. *Greyhound*'s captain made it clear that Matthew was welcome to go aboard straight away for his journey home, but Decaen ordered *Greyhound* out of Île de France the very next day. Matthew was left behind.

On 24 July the district colonel Louis Monistrol presented Matthew with papers from the French Ministry of the Marine (the French navy) issuing the instructions for his release. Matthew had learned to be suspicious and demanded to know whether the orders were really true. Monistrol assured him that they were. Matthew asked when he could leave. Monistrol told him 'as soon as circumstances allowed'. Matthew wrote to Ann, telling her excitedly that he expected to be released within the month and should be back in England in April or May 1808.

Then the war intensified. There was a British naval blockade surrounding Île de France, which led to food shortages.

Matthew became infuriated in January 1809 when he heard some news from France. Nicolas Baudin, the navigator Matthew had met when they were both sailing along the south coast of Australia, but who had since died, had become famous in France. His survey of Australia had been published, with French names given to the landmarks that Matthew had mapped as part of Britain's claim to the colony. Napoleon had paid some money towards the publication of Baudin's book. Matthew strongly suspected that this was the real reason why he had been held for so long. Now France was claiming the glory of Matthew's sightings and pretending to own British parts of Australia. He felt enraged by the French fraud and immediately wrote an angry letter to Sir Joseph Banks. He referred to the authors 'of these piracies' and complained bitterly about the loss of honour for himself and for the British nation: 'This is an injustice to our nation in general ... and to me in particular,' he raged.

In March, Matthew learned that Captain Jacques Hamelin, in the French frigate *Venus*, had moored in Île de France. Matthew knew Captain Hamelin well from their meetings in Port Jackson in 1802, when Hamelin was accompanying Baudin on their sister ship, *Naturaliste*, but Hamelin did not visit Matthew.

In August a British ship waited to take exchanged British prisoners of war to the Cape of Good Hope in South Africa. Two hundred freed prisoners went on board, but not Matthew. The ship left.

~ Nine ~

On 28 January 1810 the British ship *Harriet* arrived on Île de France again for an exchange of prisoners. It was already 18 months after the time Matthew had told Ann to expect him in England. At the last minute Matthew was told that he could leave three days later. Irritatingly, General Decaen would not give Matthew his last logbook, despite being asked repeatedly for it. Matthew assumed that Decaen had taken copies of some of the entries and used them to justify his imprisonment to the French government. Matthew was only too aware that he'd been in captivity for 'six years, five months and twenty-seven days' during which time he hadn't even been allowed to copy his log. Why would Decaen want to keep it? Matthew, churning with a confusion of emotions, quickly gathered up his belongings, said his goodbyes to the many friends he'd made, and wrote to others he had no time to visit. He felt a great fondness for the people who had helped him: 'never, in any place, or amongst any people, have I seen more hospitality and attention to strangers', he wrote.

Harriet was delayed for three months by the British naval blockade, but on 8 May Matthew felt elated to finally board the ship. 'I at length had the inexpressible pleasure of being out of reach of General Decaen,' he wrote. But did he feel a tug in his chest? He was leaving without his 'faithful companion' Trim.

Matthew learned that *Harriet* was actually bound for India, so the next day he transferred to another ship, *Otter*, that was anchored in the bay. We can only guess at his relief at joining a ship going straight to England, via the Cape of Good Hope in South Africa. But Matthew didn't go straight to England.

When, after a month, *Otter* anchored in Simon's Bay, South Africa, a vice-admiral in the British Navy in Cape Town sent a message to Matthew calling him to his office. Vice-Admiral Albemarle Bertie wanted Matthew to tell him all about Île de France. Bertie was planning to capture it with a British naval fleet. While Matthew was giving Bertie the information, 'Otter the ship sailing for England was just then going out of the bay'. There was no other ship leaving for six weeks. Matthew was stuck.

He spent his time writing pages of notes about Île de France, with drawings of landing places. By late August Vice-Admiral Bertie was satisfied that he had obtained all the useful information Matthew could supply. A few months after Matthew left Cape Town Bertie invaded and captured Île de France on behalf of Britain.

The next ship to leave for England was *Olympia*, which Matthew described as 'an indifferent sailing vessel, very leaky, and excessively ill found' – unsound and faulty. It arrived in Portsmouth on 24 October 1810. How must Matthew have felt to step onto British soil for the first time in nine and a quarter years?

Sir Joseph Banks had written to Ann telling her that Matthew was on his way. But Ann, her half-sister Isabella Tyler, and her mother, Anne Tyler, had already read in the local newspaper that a ship had arrived 'having on board Capt'n Flinders'.

'We read it again and again. Could it be true?' Isabella wrote. Ann, Isabella and Mrs Tyler were beside themselves with excitement. Ann immediately took a coach to London. Matthew took the overnight mail coach from Portsmouth. Arriving early, he took rooms in a London hotel, then visited a friend who told him that Ann was in town. Stopping off at the Admiralty he discovered that he had been promoted to captain, the rank above commander. Hurrying back to the hotel at midday, he found Ann there. Matthew hadn't received a letter from her for over four years. She was nearly 40 years old, and was looking at a white-haired man who looked much older than his 37 years. They were overwhelmed with joyful emotion.

Their rented lodgings in London buzzed with activity as they saw friends and colleagues and received many callers. The Admiralty, having promoted Matthew to captain, paid him from the time when he had left Île de France, on 8 May 1810. Now that he was back on land he received half-pay to live on. Feeling badly treated, he urged the Admiralty to date his promotion and pay to the time of his capture on Île de France in December 1803, especially considering his suffering on the island. But they wouldn't agree. To the Admiralty's way of thinking he had failed to complete his survey of the whole coast of Australia as instructed, then he had disappeared for seven years. Matthew felt keenly that his contribution to naval exploration wasn't being properly recognised and rewarded. Sir Joseph Banks did not even recommend him to become a Fellow of the Royal Society, which he had done for Captain Cook and Captain Bligh.

Matthew had at least been left a legacy of £600 from his father's will (£90,000 today), and £200 from his uncle (£30,000). Lincolnshire was calling the couple. In Matthew's home town of Donington they rejoined old friends and their families. Everyone was thrilled to see Matthew again. They were all eager to hear his stories of adventure and of his imprisonment on Île de France.

After six weeks of visiting loved ones, Ann and Matthew returned to London so that Matthew could be near the Admiralty, Sir Joseph Banks and his book publishers. He started writing up the account of his explorations straight away, with help from Banks, several illustrators, *Investigator*'s talented artists and his brother Samuel.

In 1811 Ann became pregnant. She gave birth to a baby girl on 1 April 1812. Matthew and Ann were overjoyed, and called their daughter Anne, which was the tradition in Ann's family. One generation was named Anne with an 'e', and the next was named Ann without an 'e'. In July 1812 Matthew wrote his will, as he was now a family man.

By October Matthew had sent the 200-page introduction to his book, *A Voyage to Terra Australis*, to his publisher. He wanted to call the land Australia 'as being more agreeable to the ear', but Sir Joseph Banks insisted on 'Terra Australis', the name that Matthew had used in his journals. This was taken from an earlier term used in the 1400s, *Terra Australis Incognita*, meaning the 'unknown southern land'. Once his books were published, the name Australia became the one everybody used, taken from the title of his map of the continent: *General Chart of Terra Australis or Australia*.

Matthew spent his time carefully checking the engravings of his charts and examining the proofs of his texts, tables and illustrations. He corrected and returned copies to his publisher, labouring intensely every day until all the work was done.

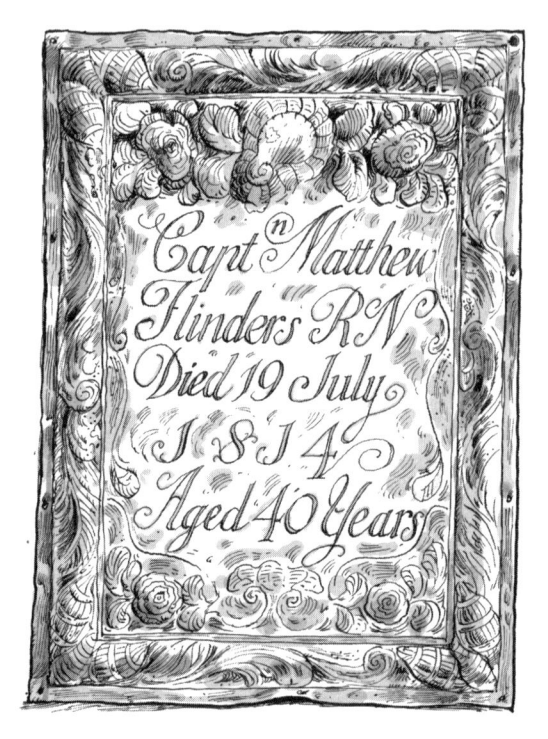

Ten

The winter of 1813 to 1814 was especially cold. Ann struggled to keep their rented rooms warm with wood fires burning in all the grates. Snow fell daily and icicles hung from the eaves of the buildings. In February 1814, Matthew's illness returned, causing him to suffer 'much pain all day'. He called for a surgeon, who passed a rubber rod into his bladder on five occasions to try to break up a supposed bladder stone. A second doctor gave him onion water, leek water, and herbal and made-up medicines. The pain worsened; some days he was in agony. He was given 'syrup of white poppies', which probably contained opium, a strong and addictive painkiller. At most he could only write for half an hour, then he had to lay down, feeling exhausted. The only thing that helped was large quantities of hot black tea.

Over the weeks Matthew became feverish, pale and weak. In May Robert Fowler, Matthew's second-in-command on *Investigator*, visited and wrote that Matthew was 'looking miserable. I don't think long for this world'. He went off his food completely and started to drift in and out of consciousness. Ann was desperately worried. In a letter to Matthew's friend Thomas Pitot in Île de France, she described Matthew 'with grey hair and sunken cheeks … he looked seventy years of age and was worn to a skeleton'.

By early July Matthew knew he was going to die. His brother Samuel visited. Matthew took his hand, looked at him fondly and simply said, 'Goodbye Samuel.'

Matthew was at last shown the three volumes of his published books, but on the following day, 19 July 1814, he took his last breath. Isabella, Ann's half-sister, was the first to go into his room. 'There lay the corpse ... placid & at rest,' she wrote. Isabella ran upstairs to fetch Ann. 'She was soon in the room of death & pressed his cold lips to hers – it was a heart breaking effort.' He was 40 years old.

Matthew was buried in St James's churchyard on Hampstead Road, north London. Ann with little Anne, aged two years, travelled back to their rooms at 14 London Street, Fitzroy Square, with Isabella and Mrs Tyler, all feeling desperately sad and tearful. Ann wrote that little Anne 'felt that something very dreadful had happened, but did not know what', and was distressed at seeing her mother crying uncontrollably.

Because Matthew had not expected to die so young, he had left generous sums of money to friends and family members in his will. Ann struggled financially on her widow's pension of £90 per year from the Navy (about £7000 today). Her disappointment was made worse knowing that Captain Cook's widow received £300 per year (£23,000).

Matthew's wife Ann died in 1852 at the age of 82. The very next year the family were told by the New South Wales and Victorian governments in Australia that they were going to pay Ann £200 a year to live on. Happily their daughter Anne was able to claim the money, worth £25,600 today. She used it to provide an excellent education for her son, William Matthew Flinders Petrie (Matthew's grandson, who he never knew). Known as Flinders Petrie, Matthew's grandson became such a famous archaeologist that he was called 'the father of archaeology'. Anne would have been astounded if she could have looked into the future to see how her son's education would help find Matthew's body after 205 years.

Isabella, Ann's half-sister, visited Matthew's grave in 1859, 45 years after his death, but the churchyard had been closed to burials when the new Euston Railway Station first took over the land. The gravestones had all been stacked together around the walls and under a big tree. Isabella looked everywhere but couldn't find Matthew's grave or his gravestone. What a sense of loss she must have felt. Was he lost forever?

William Flinders Petrie couldn't have known that his pioneering method of exploring burial sites in Egypt would be used to find his grandfather's grave 150 years later. His technique involved a precise method of searching carefully through the soil, rather than the previous crude way of digging up shovelfuls of earth until something interesting was struck.

In 2019 London archaeologists digging a new railway line behind Euston Station unearthed

Matthew's grave, identified from its battered but preserved lead coffin plate. They sent Matthew's remains for examination to find out more about his cause of death, his diet and medicines. Much of the information would have been stored in his bones. When the inspection is finished, he will be reburied in Donington where he was born. He will be laid to rest with other members of his family in the parish church of St Mary and the Holy Rood.

As for Trim, Matthew didn't have time to 'raise a monument' to him, but many others have. Today there are six statues of Trim in Australia, England and Mauritius, more than for any other cat in the world. One is at Euston Station, near Matthew's old grave.

When Matthew reaches his final resting place, perhaps there will be the statue that Matthew promised his 'most affectionate friend' beside him, inscribed with Matthew's chosen words: 'Peace be to his shade and Honour to his Memory.'

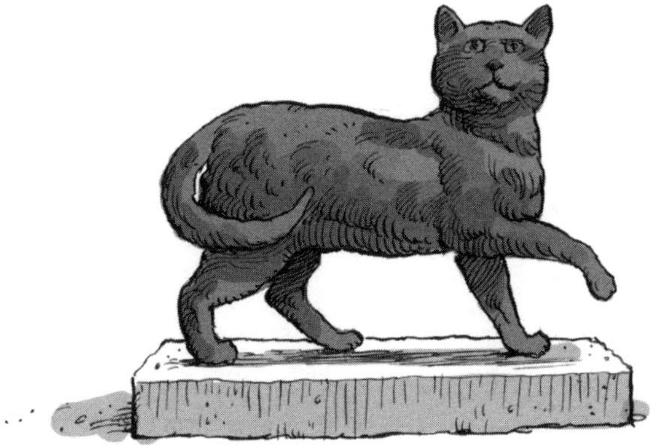

ABOUT THE AUTHOR

Ruth was born near Bournemouth beach, Dorset. Ever afterwards she was drawn to the ocean.

At the age of two years she became a Ten Pound Pom with her family – émigrés to Australia on the Assisted Passage Scheme. Five criss-crossings later her parents decided that Australia was home.

She trained as a nurse in Melbourne, taking a position as ship's nurse on a chaotic Greek passenger liner in 1969. Believing she could improve on the incompetent doctor's performance, she qualified as a doctor in the UK in 1978. Further training led to obstetrics and gynaecology, then general practice. This she enjoyed until 2018, albeit working on cruise ships in her holidays for 12 years.

A cat lover, she was in the National Maritime Museum, Greenwich, researching pest control by ships' cats, when she was handed Matthew Flinders' *Biographical Tribute to the Memory of Trim*. Thrilled by her discovery, she decided their story had to be told for children in modern English.

She lives in London by the Regent's Canal with her husband and an RSPCA foster cat, very like Trim.

ABOUT THE ILLUSTRATOR

David Parkins was born in Brighton but, like Matthew Flinders, spent most of his early life in Lincolnshire.

He has illustrated many children's picture books and fiction titles for publishers in the UK, US, Canada and France. He worked for the UK comics *Beano* and *The Dandy* for many years, drawing, among other characters, *Dennis the Menace* and *Desperate Dan*.

His editorial work includes illustrations for magazines including *Nature*, *The Economist* and *Bloomberg Businessweek*. He also creates political cartoons, which have appeared in *The Guardian*, *The Observer* and, in Canada, *The Globe and Mail* and *The Toronto Star*.

In 2006, he emigrated with his family and a couple of cats to Canada, but continues to work for UK publishers and publications as well as Canadian ones. Those original UK cats, being already fairly ancient in 2006, have since died and been replaced by three Canadian cats. One of those (Arthur – a ridiculously intelligent black-and-white cat) was born feral, in the wood shed, but is now as comfortable an indoor cat as you could wish to meet.